The
Blessings
of
Freedom

Other books by Steven C, Smith

The Reversion

The Revival

The Renewal

An Appeal to Heaven

The
Blessings
Of
Freedom

Book V of the
Stonemont Series

Steven C. Smith

As before, and for always, for my wife and children.

You are the loves of my life,

And the reasons for all my efforts.

"Those who expect to reap

The Blessings of Freedom,

must, like men,

undergo the fatigues

of supporting it. "

-Thomas Paine

From the Author

When I started writing *The Reversion*, the first book of the Stonemont series, I did so as a personal exercise to better organize the advice I was giving people about preparedness and survival by putting it in story form. I had no intention of writing a book.

As the story grew in my mind to answer an increasing number of questions, new situations presented themselves requiring more answers – which presented new situations requiring more answers, which presented new situations, which ... well, you get the idea.

I wrote it by pecking out characters individually on my phone in its notes program because, first, I do much of my writing in rather strange places (you'd be surprised) and second, I can't type. I still write that way.

As the story progressed, I kept writing ... and writing ... and writing - and it wasn't long before the story itself started becoming interesting to me and I found myself wondering what would happen next.

Yes, I know that sounds strange. I know you're supposed to have an outline and rough drafts and first drafts and subsequent polishes and all that (I seem to recall one of my high school English teachers saying something like that when I momentarily awakened from one of my mid-afternoon naps), but that's just not how I write.

Finally, after about a year, I reached a point I thought might be a good place to stop, so I did.

After doing a final read-through to catch typos (I caught most, but not all), I designed the cover and sent it all off to Amazon Create Space for printing.

I ordered a few copies, one for my wife (who I figured *had* to say she liked it), one for my mother (who I figured would enjoy seeing that her son who had failed English class had his name on the front of an actual book) and one for each of the kids, who I hoped would get a kick out of seeing it when they got older.

Then I forgot about it.

A few weeks later, something made me check my Create Space account to see if anyone may have actually bought a copy. After quite a bit of frustration (due to my extremely limited computer skills), I stumbled across the sales page and stared at it, stunned. Someone had actually bought a copy! Not only that, but hundreds of others had bought copies! The sales were coming in from all over the U.S., Canada, Australia and Europe!

I thought there had to be a mistake and waited for an email from Amazon advising me of their mix-up, but the email never came, and the sales kept growing.

Pretty soon, I happened to come across the book's page on Amazon (again, totally by accident) and saw all the reviews. Apparently, people around the world disagreed with my English teacher and liked it! Who would have thought?

I enjoyed reading the reviews (who doesn't like to hear people saying nice things about their work, right?) until one struck me: they said they couldn't wait to see what happened next!

NEXT? What next? I had never thought about a *next*. Did that mean another book?

As I watched the sales climb for *The Reversion*, I started thinking about a sequel. That seemed pretty strange, as it would imply that I would be an actual writer. When my wife would call me a writer, I just shook my head. *I'm not a writer – I'm just a guy who wrote a book.* I didn't know if there was another one in me.

Well, *The Revival* came next, then *The Renewal*, then *An Appeal to Heaven*, and now the one you are holding in your hand (I hope you're not reading it over someone's shoulder), *The Blessings of Freedom.*

I guess maybe I am now a writer.

Writing the Stonemont series has been one of the greatest pleasures of my life. Another pleasure has been hearing from so many readers from all over the world, either by email, mail, or through my YouTube and Patreon channels, *Integrative Preparedness* and *American Reversion.*

I thank each and every one of you for being a part of this great adventure – all of you *"Stonemonters"* – and I hope to keep seeing you on the rest of the journey.

I hope you enjoy *The Blessings of Freedom*, and I assure you that I am now busily writing the next book!

All the Best, and Semper Paratus!
Steve

The
Blessings
Of
Freedom

1

Augustus Carpenter tightened the strap on his bedroll and placed it on top of the rest of his gear by the door. Charlotte and Savannah were still asleep in the loft, their gentle breathing barely audible in the otherwise silent cabin, but he hadn't been able to sleep at all, thinking about the past month and the day ahead.

Quietly opening the door, he stepped out onto the front porch and took a deep breath of cool air. It seemed crisper than back home, and he could feel the freshness of the coming fall as he looked around the commons.

The first faint light of pre-dawn made it look as if the area was in dark water, the coming light not having yet lifted the shades of grey to reveal the vibrant colors announcing the approaching autumn, and the large central hall looked like a battleship appearing out of the mist surrounded by its battle group of cabins.

He saw a light in the main house, evidence of Jim's early rising, then another came on in the cabin Saw and Tuck were sharing. The lights made him feel both good and bad - good, in that they alleviated the sense of solitude he had suddenly felt, and bad because they announced the day he had been trying not to think about.

The past month had been more fulfilling than any he could remember, and the time he had been able to spend with Mike more meaningful than he would have imagined. The years, the frustrations, the disappointments and the regrets of the past had dissolved into a present filled with appreciation, respect and, finally, a profound expression of a deep and formerly unexpressed love between him and his youngest son. A family fragmented by anger and pride had been reunited by understanding because the world had fallen apart. He knew that there was a lesson in that, and he was extremely grateful for it.

He looked at the dark cabin next to his, wishing that a light would come on to show him that Mike was awake, when Mike's voice came to him from the shadows of the cabin's front porch.

"Mornin' dad."

He felt himself give a start, then flooded with a warmth he had only recently rediscovered. "Good morning, son."

"You're up early."

Augustus nodded, stepping off his own porch and walking toward where he could now see Mike sitting in a rocking chair. "I couldn't sleep."

"Me neither. Jim ought to be out in a bit to put coffee on, but we can sit here and watch for him if you want."

Augustus stepped up onto the porch and sat down in the chair next to Mike's. "Sounds good."

They sat quietly for several minutes, neither wanting to break a silence they felt was holding the inevitable at bay. Finally, Augustus spoke.

"This has been an amazing trip, Mike. It's unbelievable what you've done here." He looked at his son. "I wish we didn't have to go back so soon."

Mike nodded. "I know. It was good to have you here."

Augustus looked at his son closely. "Do you think you'll be able to come home ... I mean back, for a visit any time soon? There are a lot of people who would like to see you."

4

Mike thought for a moment and shook his head. "I don't know. I'd like to, but I think we're going to have our hands full here pretty soon. We're going to have a meeting after you all leave and discuss how we want to handle things."

He looked at his dad. "The messenger service you and Jim worked out will help a lot. I'll send a letter to you all every month to let you know how things are going here."

Augustus nodded. "That would be great. And we'll send them your way too." He smiled. "I imagine your mother will send you so many you'll get tired of reading them."

He looked around the commons, now able to see things a bit more distinctly, then back at his son. "You've built an exceptional force here in the short time you've had."

Mike shrugged. "We have good people and we've been fortunate, but I think we're going to need a lot more."

Augustus leaned forward in his chair. "Your brothers brought something up to me last night that I told them I'd ask you about."

Mike waited in silence, watching his father closely.

Augustus looked toward the other cabin, then back at Mike. "They said they've learned things from you while we've been here that they hadn't learned at The Citadel or in the Army. They said they were important things and they were wondering whether one of them could stay here for a while with some of our troops and learn from you."

Mike looked at his father, surprised at both the statement and the request. He nodded. "That would be fine with me, but it's really Jim's call."

Augustus nodded. "I understand. I'll talk to him about it, but I wanted to see if it was okay with you first. I wouldn't ask him if it wasn't."

Mike looked down at his boots stretched out in front of him. To have one of his brothers here with him for a while would be great. To know that the brothers he had

5

always looked up to wanted to learn from him was a feeling he couldn't quite identify. He shrugged. "That would be fine with me."

Augustus looked at his son seriously. "You've become an impressive man, Mike. I say that as someone who has dealt with many impressive men." He looked out into the gradually lightening commons, then back at Mike. "I will always regret that it was not I who helped you become what you are."

Mike looked at his father again, thinking about the years they had been estranged and the years before that. He remembered his initial feelings of shame and isolation when he left The Citadel. He remembered boot camp. He remembered Assessment and Selection and the missions that had tested him physically, mentally, and emotionally. He thought about the collapse and what he had done since. "You *are* the one who helped me, dad. All of the other things were just opportunities for me to understand and finally measure up to what you taught me and the standards you set for me all my life."

He looked at his boots again, shaking his head. "Every time I met an obstacle, I heard you telling me I could beat it. Every time I was confused about something, I heard you telling me the right thing to do. When I wanted to quit one time, I heard you telling me I wasn't a quitter, and I never wanted to quit again."

He looked back at his dad. "*You* made me, dad - you and mom. Everything else just gave me the chance to practice the things you taught me."

Augustus looked at Mike, replaying his son's words in his mind and wanting to believe them, but the years apart had taken their toll and it was difficult for him to fully accept it. Still, the words themselves filled him with an emotion that he struggled to control.

A second light came on at the house and kitchen door opened.

Mike stood up. "Well, that means coffee will be ready in a few minutes for the early risers. Shall we get Saw-Tuck and go get a cup?"

Augustus smiled and nodded, rising to his feet and following Mike to the brothers' cabin where Mike knocked on the door.

The door opened after a minute and Tuck stood there shirtless, brushing his teeth.

Mike chuckled. "You guys ready for a cup of coffee? The sun's almost up."

Tuck nodded and turned his head. "Hey Saw! Coffee's ready!"

"Alright!" came Saw's voice from inside. "Give me a minute!"

Mike and Augustus waited until Saw and Tuck came out, then they all started walking toward the house.

"You always get up this early?" asked Tuck, looking at his younger brother.

Mike shrugged. "That depends. Sometimes I'm just getting in about this time."

"Did dad tell you what we wanted to ask you?"

Mike nodded, looking back and forth between his brothers. "Yeah. I'd love to have you stay. Either of you. But it's Jim's call."

Tuck nodded. "We understand."

"But we'd love to, Mike," said Saw. "Both of us would. We've learned a lot from you – a lot we could use back home. Just to let you know."

"Well, just my luck," came Jim's voice from the veranda. "Four Carpenters headed my way and I've got nothing that needs building or fixing."

Mike laughed. "Morning, Jim. You ready for company?"

Jim smiled. "I'm always ready for company who drink real coffee and don't expect some kind of latte´ thing."

Augustus chuckled. "No latte´ lovers in this bunch."

Jim shook his head. "I didn't think so. The water's heating up, so it'll just be few minutes. How did you all sleep?"

"I have to admit that I laid awake a while," said Augustus, stepping up onto the veranda. "I want to thank you for your hospitality. It's been an amazing visit, and as much as I look forward to getting home, I regret having to leave."

Jim nodded. "It's been a pleasure for us too. We'll be sorry to see you go."

He glanced at Mike. "I'm still half expecting to hear that Mike wants to go back with you."

Mike shook his head. "No. I'll go back for a visit when I can, but you're stuck with me."

Jim smiled. "Good. I was hoping so."

"There is something I wanted to ask you, Jim." said Augustus.

Jim looked at him with interest. "What's that?"

Augustus looked at his sons, then back at Jim.

"We've been impressed with what we've seen here, and especially your scout program. Saw and Tuck have both told me that they've learned things from Mike that were far beyond what they learned during their own time in service, and that they would like to be able to include those skills in our own training at Les Chenes."

He again looked at his sons, then back at Jim. "I know that this might be an imposition, but I was wondering if it would be possible for one of them to stay here a while longer, along with some of their senior people, in order to train under Mike for a while. I'm not sure what compensation I could give you, but I would be agreeable to anything you suggest."

Jim looked at Augustus, thinking. The Carpenters were good folks, and their militia was comprised of quality people. Such an arrangement could be good for everyone as they worked toward establishing a cross-country

8

network between them. In fact, a regular exchange program between the two communities could prove invaluable in the areas of communications, trade, and the possible development of a mutual assistance network. "That would be fine with me, Augustus, and I can't see why there would be any need for compensation. What benefits you benefits us."

He looked at Mike. "Not to put you in a tough spot, buddy, but what do you think?"

Mike looked between Jim and his father and nodded. "I'd love to have one of them here for a while and I think we could do some good training they could take back with them." He nodded. "I'm for it."

Jim heard the water begin to boil and turned to remove the large coffee pot from the rocket stove. Setting it on the warmer, he took five cups down from the shelf above and spooned a heaping teaspoon of Folgers instant into each, giving each a stir before picking up his own and turning back around. "Grab your coffee and let's sit down."

The Carpenter men each picked up a cup and followed Jim to the table where they took their seats.

Jim sat down at the head of the table and took a long slurp of his coffee, drawing air in with the scalding liquid in order to cool it. He chuckled. "Kelly hates it when I do that."

The Carpenters all took loud slurps, causing Jim to chuckle again before he took one more of his own.

He looked at Augustus. "I'll see your offer and raise you one."

Augustus noted how Jim had changed the tone of his request to an offer.

Jim set his cup down. "How about if one of your sons stays here for a while with some of your militia and one of our scout teams go back with you? At the end of whatever length of time Mike thinks is right, the teams could switch, with your other son coming up for a while and the first going home. Scout teams would switch, too."

Augustus nodded slowly, thinking. The proposal will allow both Saw and Tuck to spend time with Mike, and Mike to be able to have family with him again - something he suspected was part of Jim's underlying purpose. It would also help to build a strong bond between Stonemont and Les Chenes as teams from each were hosted by the other, as well as begin to reinforce regular communication between them.

He nodded. "That would be quite an endeavor, Jim. I'd be for it."

Jim looked at Mike. "What do you think, Mike?"

Mike nodded enthusiastically. "I think that's a great idea."

Jim picked his cup back up and took a sip, thinking, then looked at Mike. "How long would it take you to get a team ready to go?"

Mike shrugged. "In an emergency, a few minutes, in a hurry, a few hours, but it would be better if I had another day or two."

Jim looked at Augustus. "Could you put off leaving until tomorrow or the next day?"

Augustus looked around at his sons, suddenly feeling more relaxed. He nodded and smiled. "I'll tell Charlotte to unpack her toothbrush."

He looked back at Jim. "I'm sorry to put this to you on such short notice. It just came up between us last night and I just mentioned it to Mike before we walked over here."

Jim waved the thought away, chuckling. "It's no problem. We do things on the fly a lot around here. It keeps us nimble and fluid."

He looked at Mike. "Who do you want to send back with your dad?"

10

Mike leaned back in his chair, thinking. "Well, Alex and Aaron are our two most experienced team leaders, but they've already been out twice. Brandon is good, and he's always kind of been in the shadow of the Cools. Maybe we should give him a chance."

Jim nodded. "That's fine with me."

"I don't mean to stick my nose where it clearly doesn't belong," said Saw, "but could I make a suggestion?"

Mike looked at him and nodded. "Sure. What is it?"

Saw leaned forward. "Have you noticed how Savannah and Aaron always seem to be buzzing around each other?"

Mike shook his head. "No."

"I have," said Augustus. "Like a couple of bumblebees."

He smiled. "And I've noticed that Savannah has been a little off her feed the last couple of days at the thought of leaving."

A look of understanding crept onto Mike's face. "You mean they're sweet on each other?"

Augustus chuckled. "I'd say so."

"Having Aaron lead your team on this one would probably make those two very happy," said Tuck.

Mike looked back and forth between his father and Jim, finally looking at Jim. "What do you think?"

Jim shrugged. "I have no problem with it, but I wouldn't want to send a potential problem into your dad's house."

Mike looked at Augustus. "What do you think, dad?"

Augustus smiled, liking the sound of the word and the idea. "I have no problem with it either. Savvy has already said no to just about every guy around. It might be good to bring a little fresh blood into the mix."

Jim took a sip of his coffee. "It could cause a problem, though. If they got serious and wanted to get together for good, one of us would be losing someone important to us."

Augustus looked at him and nodded. "That's true, but should we be basing our decision on that?"

Jim thought for a moment and shook his head. "No, we shouldn't."

He looked at Mike and nodded. "It's your call, but it's okay with me."

Mike picked up his coffee cup and took a long sip, thinking, then set it back down on the table and nodded. "Okay, seems like the least I can do for my little sister and a top scout. Aaron it is."

He looked at Jim. "We should be able to get the teams ready in a day or two. Is that alright?"

Jim nodded. "It's fine with me." He looked at Augustus. "Will that work for you?"

Augustus nodded. "Sure, if it's not an imposition."

Jim shook his head. "Not a bit. We're expecting Ken Dehmer to bring some of his Rangers by tomorrow. This will give you a chance to meet them."

Augustus nodded again. "Excellent. Thank you."

He looked at Saw and Tuck. "We'd better go tell your mother and sister to unpack some things."

Draining his cup and standing up, he raised the empty cup toward Jim. "Thank you, Jim. Again, you've made us feel like family."

Jim stood up and smiled. "I figure you are, Augustus, so breakfast will be ready about an hour after eastern tree-top. Don't be late."

Augustus chuckled. "Carpenters are never late for chow."

Jim walked to the edge of the veranda as he heard them wash their cups in the wash basin, then raised his own cup to them as they stepped off the veranda to walk back to their cabins.

The sun was sending its first rays of the day through the trees to the east, making them look like dark lace against the orange and purple sunrise, and a cool breeze blew from the northeast, reminding him that autumn had arrived.

He walked back to the warming stove and made himself a second cup of coffee, thinking.

A letter in yesterday's mail from Ken Dehmer had said that Dehmer would be coming by tomorrow to touch base, and the visit was coming at an opportune time. The newly formed Kansas Rangers were still small, made up mostly of former Kansas State troopers, but their existence sent an important message that law and order were to be reestablished in the areas controlled by the new confederation. Hopefully, they would develop a reputation that would draw other quality people to want to join them, just as the Texas Rangers had.

Thought of the Rangers made him think about the situation in Texas. Declan's visit had been brief due to the growing threat coming out of New Mexico, and he had expressed his concern that the fledgling Army of Texas might not be able to deploy enough men to secure the western Texas border. That meant that Lubbock and Amarillo could be in jeopardy, and with them the entirety of west Texas.

He sat back down and took a long sip of his coffee, thinking.

Texas was the main buffer, the main protection, against what had been reported by Declan to be a strengthening push of the Reconquista out of the southwest. If Texas didn't hold, there was little to keep the expansion of the new Aztlan from expanding through Oklahoma and western Kansas, and that brought it close to the confederation. To make things even more complicated, Mahoney's information indicated the possibility of an equally dangerous threat from the north.

13

The sunrise now shot streaks of pink above the lightening purples and oranges, and he continued to sip his coffee as he watched the dark lace of the trees fade to reveal themselves in the growing light. It promised to be a beautiful day and he held onto the beauty as he finished the cup.

Finally draining the last sip, he rose and took the cup to the wash basin where he washed it out and placed it in the drying rack. Turning to the ready room, he took his dark brown Resistol from a peg and set it on his head, then took a rifle from the rack, gave the magazine base a smack out of habit, chambered a round and set it on safe. Slinging it so it hung muzzle down on his right side, he stepped off the veranda and headed toward the newly finished stable.

It was light enough now that he was able to see the ground as he walked down the path toward the barn, now used for storage since the store had been moved to Jamestown. A rooster crowed from the chicken houses farther down the path and he turned onto the side path that went around the barn to the stable.

Several lights were on at the stable, indicating that someone was there earlier than usual, and he saw movement through one of the windows as he approached, though the main stable doors were still closed. Entering through the pedestrian door next to the tack room, he scanned the rows of stalls, finally seeing a young man emerge from one on the end pushing a wheelbarrow and whistling.

"You're up early, son."

The young man jerked his head up at Jim's voice, startled. "Sorry, sir. I mean yes sir, Mr. Wyatt."

Jim smiled and walked toward him. "I didn't think there would be anyone here this early."

14

The young man set the wheelbarrow down on its legs and straightened up. "There's not usually, sir. I just came in early to have a little time alone with the horses."

Jim stopped a few feet from him. "You like horses, do you?"

The young man smiled. "Oh, yes sir. I like them better than people, sometimes."

Jim chuckled. "Sometimes, so do I. What's your name, son?"

"Ryan, sir."

"How long have you worked here, Ryan?"

"Almost six months, sir."

"You like it?"

Ryan's smile widened. "Oh, yes sir. My friends all want to be scouts, but I like working with the horses."

He looked down self-consciously. "They think I'm a little strange, but I don't think so."

Jim thought for a minute and shook his head. "No, neither do I. Would you mind saddling Ghost for me?"

Ryan nodded. "Sure, Mr. Wyatt, right away."

Jim walked to the large rolling doors at the west end of the stable and pushed them open. The sun had risen to the point where it was starting to light up the valley and he could see to the next rise of wooded hills several miles away. A mixed herd of cattle and bison grazed in the fields below and the last bit of darkness had left the western sky to create a brilliant blue dome above.

He stood there for several minutes, enjoying the peace and beauty until he heard the hoof steps of Ghost coming up behind him.

"Here you are, Mr. Wyatt," said Ryan.

He patted the horse's neck. "I can tell he's excited to get out for a while." He handed the reins to Jim.

Jim took the reins in his left hand and smoothed his right hand down Ghost's neck. "Good mornin', buddy. Ready to go for a walk?"

Ghost turned his head into Jim and gave a soft blow.

"He's ready, sir," said Ryan, smiling. "I can see it."

Jim stepped back a bit, gently stroking the horse's forehead and looking into the intelligent eyes. "Is that right, boy? Are you ready to go out for a bit?"

Ghost gave another soft blow and put his muzzle under Jim's outstretch arm.

Jim chuckled and led the horse out of the stable, followed by Ryan.

Throwing the right rein over the horse's neck and gathering in with the other in his left hand, he grabbed the pommel, put his foot in the stirrup and swung up into the saddle. He settled the rifle down his side and looked down at Ryan. "You said all of your friends want to be scouts?"

Ryan nodded. "Yes, sir. Pretty much."

"Why?"

Ryan shrugged. "They think it sounds exciting."

Jim nodded. "I suppose it does. Have any of them joined?"

Ryan nodded. "A couple of them have. The rest are trying to talk their parents into it or waiting to get old enough to join."

Jim again looked out over the valley and nodded as if to himself. Trouble was coming and young men were waiting to be old enough or trying to talk their parents into letting them join because it sounded like an adventure to them. It seemed like the Revolutionary War or the War Between the States all over again. He wondered how young men ever got to be old men with the world always so ready to give them opportunities to die.

He looked back down at Ryan. "You tell your friends that we just might need them, but that they shouldn't look forward to it too much. There are a great many things more fulfilling than fighting."

Ghost danced a step, anxious to get going, but Jim held him in place, still looking at Ryan. "And we're going to need you here with our horses. Okay?"

Ryan looked up at Jim, sensing something serious that he didn't quite understand. He nodded. "Yes sir, Mr. Wyatt. I'll be here."

Jim held Ghost through another dance, still looking at Ryan, then nodded and wheeled the horse toward the trail that led to the valley floor.

He gave the horse its head on the descending switchback until they reached the valley floor, then took it to the canter he knew it was eager for.

The air was cool, and the long strides of the big horse brought a welcome chill to his face. If he hadn't been fully awake before, the cool wind and invigorating rhythm brought him up a couple of notches and he headed across the valley to the wooded hills in the distance.

Cattle and bison looked up with mild interest as he passed, and he settled into the comfortable rocking of the gait as Ghost's lengthening strides ate up the distance.

Thoughts of young men fighting for freedom and adventure filled his mind and he tried to push them away, but Ryan's face kept coming back to him, as did Aedan's and Brody's. Young men, boys really, whose futures should be filled with opportunities, families and fulfillment, not spent fighting other young men, killing and being killed to further the causes of others.

The thoughts angered him, and he realized that he had let Ghost go to a full gallop that had brought them to the line of hills sooner than he had expected. Easing off, he brought Ghost back to a canter, then to a trot and then to walk as he scanned the hills in front of him.

The line of hills contained portions of the land holds selected by Christian, the Garners, the Murphys and Mike. Each included a wide section of hills, gradually narrowing in their "pie slice" to a point near Jamestown.

17

Thus situated, each parcel contained wooded hills, pastures and a portion of the large creek that ran along the base of the hills - everything to make each family self-sufficient. Additionally, several oil wells were located on Christian's holding, the production of which Christian intended to share with the others.

Checking the height of the sun to see how much time he had, he turned the horse onto a path that disappeared into the trees as it wound up the hill. The air was cooler under the shade of the trees, and he again gave Ghost his head as they ascended to a saddleback, then continued up to the top of the southern ridge.

The top was almost flat, an area of about forty acres dotted with several stands of trees, and he stopped for a moment to survey it. He had only been up here once before and he had forgotten how peaceful, almost serene, it felt. He gave a gentle squeeze with his knees and Ghost moved forward at a slow walk, giving another soft blow as if happy to be moving again.

He passed through a stand of tall oaks, the ground beneath them almost devoid of underbrush due to the lack of sunlight under the canopy, and exited onto a broad, flat shelf facing the southwest. Riding to the western edge, he stopped.

The view was amazing. Miles of country spread out in front of him, so far that it was impossible for him to judge the distance. He studied the line at which the horizon met the startling blue of the sky, but it was indistinct.

He looked down at the fields and pastures far below him, dots of Stonemont cattle peppering the broad swaths of prairie grass, and an idea began to form in his mind. Looking again at the horizon, a vision began to take shape.

2

"You're late!" yelled Christian as he saw Jim approaching the house.

Jim stepped up onto the veranda, taking off his hat and unslinging his rifle. "I'm never late. You all must be early."

He hung his hat on a hook, cleared and racked the rifle, and turned back toward the table, seeing that everyone else was already seated and drinking coffee. "I got to riding and thinking and lost track of time. Sorry to keep everybody waiting."

"Remember what you told me one time?" asked Christian.

Jim looked at his nephew as he took a cup off a hook and sat down. "About what?"

"About people using the time you keep them waiting to count your faults?"

Jim squinted at him. "Yeah? Did you come up with anything?"

Christian leaned back in his chair, a self-satisfied smile on his face. "I just asked Kelly if she had a big piece of paper. I was about to get started."

Jim shook his head in mock disgust. "Well, when she brings you your crayon, you might want to start with me obviously being too easy on you in the respect for your elders department."

Bill chuckled, looking over at Augustus. "This used to be a regular morning routine for them. Looks like it's coming back."

"What's coming back?" asked Kelly, coming out of the kitchen door with a large platter of pancakes and a basket of biscuits.

"The morning duel between your husband and nephew," said Bill.

"Uh-oh," she laughed, placing the platters on the table and looking at the Carpenters. "This could go on for a while. Better get comfortable."

Jim reached for the coffee pot on the table and filled his cup. "Yeah, I imagine I could hit his softballs out of the park for a while, but we have more important things to talk about."

He looked at Kelly. "Did Augustus and Charlotte tell you they'll be staying for a few more days?"

Kelly nodded, holding the door open for Jenny to carry platters of bacon and fried eggs out to the table. "They did. Maybe we'll go into town today to check out a couple of the new shops."

She sat down next to Jim and looked at Charlotte and Savannah. "A new bakery just opened, and they say their pastries are amazing."

Tracy pushed out through the kitchen door carrying a bowl of sausage gravy in one hand and an apple pie in the other. "I don't see how they could be better than yours, but I'm willing to give it a try."

She set the gravy and pie on the table and sat down next to Mike, smiling at him. "I'm afraid you're going to be disappointed with my cooking after being used to all this."

Mike smiled back. "I bet you cook just fine."

Tracy shook her head. "I cook like a law student. Hot pockets and Chinese take-out. Now we don't have either one."

Mike chuckled and looked at Jim. "I've already told Aaron that he's going to be taking his team back to Les Chenes and to start getting ready, but I was wondering if you wanted to piggy-back a couple of other teams onto them as they go down through Missouri."

Jim took a sip of his coffee and shook his head. "The Les Chenes group will be heading back the normal route and making pretty good time. I want our other teams to be able to go as slow as they need to and explore areas we don't know." He accepted the platter of eggs from Kelly and scooped three onto his plate before passing it on. "I assume you want Brandon as the first team leader. Do you have any thoughts about a second?"

Mike nodded. "Justin Coons."

Jim looked at him for a moment, then at Christian. "I don't know him. Do you?"

Christian shook his head.

"No reason you should," said Mike, forking several rashers of bacon onto his plate. "He's quiet. Doesn't stick out or make a fuss. In fact, it took me quite a while to notice how good he was."

He passed the platter on and accepted the basket of biscuits. "He does everything right, he's smart as a fox and deadly as a cottonmouth, and all the other scouts know it. In fact, he's from down there somewhere."

"Down where?" asked Christian.

Mike shrugged. "The Ozarks somewhere."

Jim nodded. "Sounds good. Do you need to be with the teams today?"

Mike shook his head. "Not really. I can just tell Brandon and Justin to start getting their guys ready."

Jim poured maple syrup over his pancakes. "Good. Christian and I are going to run up to see Mahoney today. Since the ladies are going shopping, maybe you'd like to bring your dad and brothers along with us."

Mike looked at his dad and brothers, who all nodded. "Sounds good. Is something going on up there?"

Jim took two biscuits out of the basket and cut them open, laying each cut-side up on his plate. "We got a message that he'd like to talk to us."

He ladled gravy over the biscuits. "I didn't tell you before, but Mahoney sent me a letter right before your wedding. He said they'd picked up a refugee from up north who claimed that Muslim warlord up in Minnesota was pushing south into Iowa. He wants to talk about it."

Mike looked at him sharply. "That doesn't sound good."

Jim shook his head. "No, it doesn't."

"We don't know much about what's to the north of us," observed Christian.

Jim shook his head again. "No, we don't. Hopefully, Mahoney does. We'll see."

They ate breakfast, then split into groups as the women prepared to go into Jamestown and the men to the city.

Clouds had begun to build up in the north, occasional streaks of lightning showing in the distance, and a northern breeze kept the temperature from rising despite the bright sunshine overhead.

They made good time on the empty highways, abandoned vehicles still dotting the shoulders of the road, and they were soon approaching the outer suburbs.

Empty vehicles were thicker here, and they had to slow down several times in order to snake their way through choke points where drivers hadn't steered off the main roadway before their vehicles had come to a rest.

Driving the lead truck, the sight of an unfinished hospital gave Christian a thought and he looked at Jim who was riding shotgun. "I have an idea."

Jim looked at him, resisting the temptation to hit the softball. "What's that?"

"We're wanting to build a larger medical facility, right?"

Jim nodded. "Uh huh."

"I just remembered where we can get all of the supplies we need."

Jim looked at him with increased interest. "Yeah, where?"

"They did a regional mass casualty drill once when I was at the hospital. The emergency equipment trailers for the region were kept at a little hospital here in Overland Park." He nodded ahead. "It's just a few miles up the road."

"What's in them?"

Christian shrugged. "I'm not really sure. We never opened them, but the emergency preparedness guy said they had pretty much everything you need to set up a field hospital."

Jim looked at him with renewed interest. "And it's just up the road a bit?"

Christian nodded. "You want to stop by and check?"

Jim looked up the highway and nodded. "You bet."

They continued into the suburbs until they came to an intersection clogged by several cars that had obviously been in a collision. Taking to the shoulder of the road, Christian navigated around the vehicles and turned to the east, nodding at a low, brown brick building with a taller section on its south end. "That's it."

Jim looked at the building they were quickly approaching. On two sides of the taller section was large signage that said *Saint Luke's South Hospital*. "You been here before?"

Christian turned onto a curving side road that led to the hospital. "Just to get the trailers. I never went inside."

Jim nodded to himself and watched as they approached the hospital. The parking lots surrounding it were full of cars, some showing obvious signs of having been broken into while others simply bore the dust of time. Three flags on separate poles; one the American flag, one the flag of Kansas, and a white one with a faded purple design, hung limply, though obviously in tatters.

Turning into the hospital entrance drive, they drove around the building, passing several entrances that appeared damaged until they came around to the rear loading dock. Christian nodded at two white trailers parked side-by-side in the dock yard. "There they are."

He pulled to a stop, not entering the dockyard, and put the truck in park. "Let me go take a look at them before we pull in there."

Jim nodded as Christian stepped out of the truck, then stepped out himself, watching the roofline and the area around them. The Carpenters stepped out of the second truck and several scouts got out of the third, all holding rifles ready, with several of the scouts advancing into the dock yard to cover Christian.

Passing two open shipping containers full of construction debris, Christian walked around to the rear of the trailers. Both had had their locks torn off and been opened, allowing some of their contents to fall out onto the pavement, but both seemed to still contain most of their equipment.

He walked back around and approached Jim, who was looking up at the building with interest. "They've been opened, but it doesn't look like much, if anything, was taken. Probably because nothing could be eaten and nobody was interested in setting up a hospital."

Jim nodded, still looking at the building. "Good. What does a hospital have that we could use?"

Christian shrugged. "I don't know. I'd guess a lot of stuff. Mike would know better than me."

"About what?" Mike asked as he approached.

"Jim wants to know what a hospital would have that we could use."

Mike pushed his cap up and scratched his hairline before resetting the cap on his head. "More than we can carry right now. The drugs are probably all gone, but I bet we could fill a semi with other stuff that would be useful."

Jim looked at him. "Like what?"

Mike shrugged. "Dressings, suture kits, surgical trays, maybe even fluids ... a lot of stuff."

Jim looked back up at the building again. "Well, we won't be able to take anything with us now, but let's go in and see if there's anything worth coming back for."

Christian nodded. "You want to hook up these trailers while we're here?"

Jim shook his head. "No. I don't want to be pulling trailers around the city. We'll pick them up on the way back."

He turned back toward the truck. "Let's go in and take a look around."

Getting back into the trucks, they continued to drive around the hospital, going up a hill until they reached a circular drive surrounding a helipad. Two ambulances stood parked under a canopy that extended from the door to the helipad ramp, a sign on the canopy indicating it to be the ambulance entrance.

Christian stopped at the entrance to the drive and looked over at Jim. "I'd say this would be a good place to go in."

Jim looked around, then nodded. "Let's leave the trucks here. "I'd hate to get trapped in that circle."

Christian nodded, shut off the truck and got out, slinging his rifle around his neck.

Jim followed, as did the Carpenters and the scouts from the other trucks.

"Alpha squad, set security," shouted Mike. "The rest come with us."

The eight scouts of Alpha squad fanned out to take positions around the parking lot, several climbing into the beds of pickups to gain a better view. Mike watched and nodded. "Okay, let's go."

The automatic doors to the hospital stood open, one side hanging off its hinges, and a weather-yellowed sheet that had been caught in it ruffled in the slight breeze. Taking the lead, Mike stepped through the door into the darker interior.

He moved slowly into the unfamiliar space, careful to avoid stepping on debris that littered the floor and keeping his rifle at low ready.

The air was cool but stuffy, testament to the building having been empty for some time without functioning air handlers, and a faint chemical taste touched the back of his throat.

Coming to a door on his left that said SECURITY, he tried the handle and found it locked. Advancing another twenty feet into the interior, he stopped. A long plexiglass-faced counter ran the length of the room to his right, obviously the station for doctors and nursing staff. Across from it were a number of treatment rooms.

Hearing scouts enter behind him, he advanced to behind the counter and stopped again. Rolling chairs sat in a disorderly fashion behind the long desk on which rested telephones, computers and thick binders. Papers and food wrappers littered the floor.

Signaling the team to check the treatment rooms, he stepped through a doorway on his left into a galley kitchen and supply room. The beam of his flashlight showed bins of untouched medical supplies, though the meds cabinet was empty. Going to a back hallway, he found two locked doors, a bathroom, and what appeared to be a break room with a wall of lockers, a sink, a microwave and an empty refrigerator with the door standing open. Seeing nothing of interest, he walked back through the supply room and into the ER.

"One body in room eight, Mike," said the team leader as he walked over to him. "Everything else is clean."

Mike nodded. "Select two guys to stay here and wait for me. I'll be back in a minute."

The scout nodded as Mike walked back outside.

Squinting against the daylight after the gloom of the darkened interior, Mike exited the building and motioned to Jim, Christian, his dad and his brothers. "Entry's clear." He looked at Jim. "One body in the ER, but nothing else."

Jim nodded as he approached. "Where would the stuff be that we could use?"

"Surgery and central supply."

Jim looked at Christian. "You have any idea where those would be?"

Christian shrugged. "Surgery is usually on the main level. Central supply would probably be on the dock level, which looks like it's a level down."

Jim looked at Mike and nodded. "Okay. Let's go."

It only took them a few minutes to find the surgery department, but another fifteen to find the central supply, called the *Universal Resource Center*, and another thirty to pry the doors open with tools they found in the facilities department. When they finally got inside, they stared at the endless rows of shelves containing medical supplies.

Jim whistled under his breath as he shined his flashlight across the aisles. "Well, I guess no one else thought about setting up a hospital."

"You want to come back for it?" asked Christian.

Jim nodded, still looking around at the seemingly endless rows. "Yep. All of it."

3

Tom Mahoney looked up from the letter he was writing to see the large frame of Danny O'Brien in the doorway. It never ceased to amaze him how much space Danny took up.

"You back already?"

Danny nodded as he walked in and sat down in a chair on the other side of the table at which Mahoney was working. "Force wants to have a sit-down. He says he's getting pressure from a group to his east, and he thinks we might be able to help straighten things out."

Mahoney laid the pen down on the notepad and leaned back in his chair. "Why does he think that?"

Danny shrugged. "He thinks we're all alike, so he thinks we all must know each other and think the same way."

Mahoney shook his head and looked out the window at the city skyline several miles to the north. "I guess he's never going to change."

Danny shrugged again. "Prison mind-set."

Mahoney nodded. "Do we know who they are?"

Danny leaned back, lacing his fingers behind his head and stretching. "Not really. Just a loose bunch of dirtbags that got run out of eastern Jackson County from what I hear."

"What kind of pressure are they giving him?"

Danny gave a bigger stretch, arching his back until Mahoney heard several pops, then relaxed with his ankle crossed over his knee and his hands folded in his lap. "Just probes, mainly. He said they come across 435 and set some fires or fire a few shots into the city. Nothing major, but he thinks things are going to escalate."

Mahoney shrugged. "So, why doesn't he take care of it himself?"

"He says he's stretched pretty thin that far east, but I'm thinking he mainly just wants to use us as a hammer on his east side in order to make it look like he's got a stronger ally."

Mahoney looked out the window again. "Uh huh. Tail trying to wag the dog."

Danny nodded. "Exactly. By the way, a runner just told me that Christian is on his way in with his uncle and some other people."

Mahoney's eyebrows lifted in surprise. "Jim came with him?"

"That's what the runner said."

Mahoney thought for a moment. "Do you know where Force is right now?"

Danny nodded. "He's at the interchange. Said he'd be there all day."

Mahoney smiled. "Good. Maybe it's time we showed him a bit about our allies."

Danny lifted his chin to indicate something out the window. "Well, they're here."

Mahoney looked out the window to see one of their sentry vehicles pulling into the circle drive. Behind it followed six pickup trucks. "Looks like they brought quite a bunch. That should help."

He got to his feet. "Let's go welcome them."

Augustus gave a low whistle as he looked out the window at the large stone mansion they were stopping in front of. "I didn't think folks in the city would last through the collapse, at least not these kinds of folks."

Mike looked over at his father. "The people here now aren't the original tenants. Most of those either died, vanished or traded their houses for food and protection. The current residents are part of the group that controls most of the city now."

"How did that happen?" asked Tuck from the back seat. "I mean, how were they able to take over?"

Mike looked at his brother in the rear-view mirror. "A lot of them were on the city police and fire departments. Others were part of the city's Irish community. Tom told me that they jumped on things fast and hard when the lights went out, secured their areas and a lot of food from the grocery warehouses and pretty much hunkered down until most of the city had died off from bad water, starvation or killing each other. Then, they cleaned out what was left and started over."

"Who's Tom?" asked Tuck.

Mike nodded toward two men walking down the entry walk toward them. "That's him there, the smaller one."

Mahoney approached the circle drive and smiled. "Christian! Jim! Good to see you!"

Christian smiled back as he took Mahoney's proffered hand. "Hi, Tom. It looks like things are going well around here."

Mahoney nodded. "Can't complain. Not that it would do any good."

He looked at Jim, extending his hand. "And what gets you out of your beloved Stonemont, Jim?"

Jim shook the hand and chuckled. "My nephew told me he'd bring me up to the big city and show me the tall buildings."

Mahoney laughed. "We've got 'em, but I don't think you'd want to go in them. We sure don't."

He nodded behind them. "Looks like you've brought quite a team."

Jim looked back to see Mike leading his father and brothers toward them. "Mike's dad and brothers, out from South Carolina."

Mahoney looked surprised, stepping forward to extend his hand to Mike. "Mike, good to see you again. I hear you've brought family."

Mike shook the hand, then stepped to the side to make the introductions. "Tom, this is my dad, Augustus, and my brothers, Sawyer and Tucker. Guys, this is Tom Mahoney, the honcho around here."

Mahoney chuckled and held out his hand to Augustus. "I don't know about the honcho part, but it's good to meet you."

"And you," Augustus nodded, shaking the hand.

"And to the brothers," Mahoney said, shaking Saw and Tuck's hands. "Welcome to Little Hibernia."

Each nodded with a "thank you" and Mahoney turned back to Jim and Christian.

"We've got a load of movies and equipment ready for you, but I wanted to talk to you about that guy up north and now something else has come up, so you've come at the right time."

"What's up?" asked Christian.

Mahoney shoved his hands in his jeans pockets and lifted his chin toward the east. "We've got to go meet the guy who runs things on the east side. He's wanting us to help him with a problem he's got."

"Who is he?" asked Christian.

Mahoney curled his lip. "He goes by the name of Force. He's an ex-con who has actually stabilized the east side by laying down and enforcing rules and creating a functioning community for his people. In a way, he's been successful at it by applying even stricter laws than the ones he spent his younger days breaking."

Jim gave a sardonic smile. "Sounds like he grew as a person."

Mahoney nodded. "He did. He says he was influenced by the Black Muslims in prison and the Black Hebrew

Israelites outside. He's neither, but he lives a very disciplined life and requires the same of his followers."

"He sounds like a good one to have on your flank," said Christian.

Mahoney shrugged. "Yes and no. We don't have any problems with him, but we don't feel we could depend on him for help, either."

"Why not?" asked Jim.

"He's a separatist. He doesn't believe in the mixing of races. He keeps his people away from us, and us away from them."

Jim and Christian looked at each other, but neither commented.

"I figure he's wanting to pit us against a group he feels threatened by in order to stay out of direct contact with them, letting two groups he doesn't like fight it out for his benefit" continued Mahoney. "It makes sense from his standpoint, but we have no intention of being his hit men."

He looked at Jim and Christian and smiled. "We're heading over to meet him now. Care to come along?"

Jim and Christian looked at each other, considering the situation. Finally, Jim shrugged. "May as well."

The trip took less than ten minutes, during which time Jim and Christian observed the deterioration of areas they had both been familiar with during their time in the city years before. Although the Irish enclave around Loose Park had been kept up well, in some cases even improved, the famed Country Club Plaza and areas to the east exhibited a desolation that was usually seen only in war or the most neglected slums of the pre-collapse world.

Jim looked out at the broken windows and debris-littered streets as they drove through the Plaza, then looked at Christian. "Did you ever bring dates down here when you were younger?"

Christian nodded, taking in the deterioration around them. "Yeah. You?"

Jim nodded. "My parents came here on dates in the forties. They brought us down when we were kids to walk around and see the big Easter bunnies. My friends and I would cruise Winstead's and Sydney's drive-ins looking at girls and showing off our cars in high school, and later I brought dates down here for dinner."

He looked around, remembering. "The last girl I brought here was Kelly. We'd come down just to walk around holding hands."

Christian looked over at his uncle. "So how many years did you come down here?"

Jim thought for a moment, adding up the years. "Fifty."

"Wow."

Jim continued to look at the decay around him. "Yeah, wow."

It only took them a few more minutes travelling east before Christian saw the brake lights on the Hibernian gun truck ahead of him light up and he applied his own brakes until they crawled to a stop some fifty yards short of a roadblock constructed of assorted orange and white street department barricades.

He watched as several men with rifles came out and approached Mahoney's Ranchero at the front of the column. All three men wore black BDUs and black do-rags, and all three approached Mahoney's vehicle on the driver's side. He looked over at his uncle. "What do you think?"

Jim watched the men as they swaggered and postured, flagging each other repeatedly with their rifle muzzles as they attempted to show authority to the visiting group. "A street gang trying to play army. A clown show."

Christian nodded and looked around, surveying the area. A large parking lot with only a few cars in it was to their right. To their left were two side streets of abandoned houses and vacant lots.

Part of the barricade slid to the side and the brake lights of Mahoney's Ranchero and the gun truck went out as they moved forward toward the gate.

Christian kept his foot on the brake, studying the barricade, then looked at Jim. "You feel like going in there?"

Jim shook his head. "Nope."

"Me neither."

Jim looked around and nodded toward the parking lot. "Let's wait for them over there."

They waited in the parking lot for over an hour until the gate opened again and they saw the Hibernian vehicles exit. A wave from Mahoney indicated that he wanted them to follow him and they fell in to retrace the route through the Plaza back to the enclave around Loose Park.

A light sprinkle had started as they pulled back into Mahoney's drive and the gentle breeze of earlier had escalated to a light wind from the north that carried on it the taste of rain.

Jim watched as Mahoney got out of his Ranchero. "He doesn't look happy."

Christian watched Mahoney walk back toward them and rolled down the window. "No, he doesn't."

Mahoney stopped at Christian's door, looked around for a moment, then looked back at them seriously. "Sorry that took so long, but there may be some serious trouble headed our way."

He looked back toward the north for a moment, then back at both Christian and Jim. "If you can stay a little longer, I'd like to talk to you about it."

"So, they want to relocate somewhere out here," said Mike, refilling his cup from the coffee pot on the table, "but they don't know where."

Jim nodded, taking a sip from his own cup as he leaned back into the couch. "Sounds like it."

"What do you think?"

Jim stared out the south windows of the den, considering. Mahoney's desire to move his entire community out of the city was a surprise. Understandable, but a surprise, and it brought both possibilities and concerns to his mind – possibilities and concerns he had taken a day to think about.

He took another sip. "I can understand them wanting to move. Living in that enclave surrounded by a dead city is bound to have an effect, regardless of how much they tried to maintain their community identity. I imagine they're starting to feel the isolation and not wanting that to be their future."

Christian nodded. "I can understand that. The question is, where do they go?"

Jim looked at his nephew. "They've asked for our help, so the question is where do we *want* them to go?"

Christian looked at him for a moment, thinking about the possibilities. "Okay. Where do we *want* them to go?"

Jim got up from the couch and walked over to the windows looking out onto the commons. Some of the kids' friends from town had come over to visit and they were running around the area yelling and shrieking at the game they were playing. He smiled. "I forgot today was Saturday."

Christian chuckled. "Yeah, the days run together sometimes. How are the kids liking school?"

Jim smiled again. "They like it. They were doing well before, but kids need to be around other kids or else they just become miniature adults before they get to enjoy being kids." He raised his cup toward the playing children. "I imagine that's one of the things Mahoney has been thinking about."

Christian nodded. "Makes sense."

He got up from his couch and joined Jim to look out at the commons. "So, where do we want them?"

Jim waited for a moment before answering, still watching the children. "That's a good question." He looked at Christian. "What do you think of them?"

Christian shrugged. "They seem like good folks to me. Why? Do you see a problem?"

Jim shook his head. "No, not really. They seem like good people to me, too. My only reservation is moving a fully-formed group we don't really know into an area where they could have an effect on us."

Christian looked at him. "What do you mean?"

Jim turned toward Christian. "One of the reasons we've been successful here is that we established a core group around a shared system of beliefs and expectations, then accepted people into our community according to their acceptance of those expectations. Then, from a position of strength, we formed alliances with other groups who had similar values."

He took a sip of his coffee before continuing. "Mahoney's group is different. They're fully formed, with many of their loyalties and dynamics going back for generations. They fought hard for their survival in a way that makes their internal bonds and loyalties even stronger. They've survived an unbelievable situation against unbelievable odds and established a self-contained community answerable to no one else, which might make them hesitant to align themselves with other groups they don't know. Finally, they're city people. That doesn't make them bad, but it does make them different, and they might have a hard time acclimating to such a drastic change all at once."

Christian nodded. "Yeah, I see what you mean. So, what are you thinking?"

Jim looked to the south. "We're strong to the south with our alliances through Linn County, then to the west up through Freelove and McGregor's areas and up to Riley, so we don't need them there. To the north is where we have our current problems, so we can't put them there. It would be putting them between the hammer and the anvil when they're just getting set up."

"That leaves east," said Christian.

Jim nodded, as if picturing their eastern border in his mind. "Yep, that leaves east."

He set his cup down and walked to one of the bookcases where he took a large Rand McNally atlas from a lower shelf and returned to open it on a side table.

Leaning over, he leafed through the pages until he came to the map of Missouri and placed his finger on a spot on the Kansas-Missouri border. "This area is directly east of us on the Missouri side. It's a good mix of field and forest, with plenty of water and ringed by several mostly-abandoned small towns."

Christian looked at him. "You think the people around there would allow Mahoney's bunch to settle there?"

Jim straightened up. "Maybe not directly, but there may be a better way."

"What do you mean?"

Jim nodded at the atlas. "That area was about half in Cass County and half in Bates County. The sheriffs have solidified themselves around their county seats -

Harrisonville in Cass and Butler in Bates, and neither has the manpower or inclination to secure that area that is so far from their towns."

Christian looked confused. "How do you know that?"

"McGregor told me."

"When?"

Jim smiled. "When he asked me if we would have any interest in expanding into that area."

"You mean you already talked to them about it?" Christian asked, surprised.

Jim shrugged. "Actually, they came to us. They didn't have the ability to secure that area, but they wanted it secured. I told them that it would stretch us pretty thin, but that I'd think about it. Now we can use it."

"So, we give it to Mahoney?"

Jim shook his head. "Nope. We accept the area for Stonemont, then ask Mahoney if he would like for his people to settle in that part of our area."

Christian nodded slowly, a small smile forming on his lips. "So, Stonemont gains the territory and places a ready-made community in it that will help guard us on the east."

Jim nodded, picked up his cup of coffee and took a sip. "Exactly."

Christian nodded again, the eyes showing both appreciation and amusement. "I just remembered something."

"What's that?"

"You always used to beat me at chess."

Jim lifted his cup to hide his smile. "Really? We'll have to start playing again, then."

A knock at the door made him turn to see Kelly entering the room.

"Are you two telling secrets?" she smiled.

Jim's smile grew bigger at the sight of her. "Can't tell you."

"Why not?" she asked, walking up beside him. "I can keep a secret."

He chuckled. "So can I."

She snuggled under his outstretched arm, putting one arm around his waist and giving him a soft punch in the ribs with the other fist.

"And enhanced interrogation methods will do you no good either," he laughed. "I'm trained to resist them."

She looked up at him. "Well, I know one thing you're not trained to resist."

He smiled down at her. "Your bread pudding?"

She rolled her eyes, gave him a harder shot in the ribs with her elbow and ducked out from under his arm. "Whatever."

He laughed as she walked back to the door then watched as she turned to look at Christian.

She made a play flip of her hair. "Ken Dehmer just came through the contact gate, but don't tell your uncle, 'cause it's a secret."

He chuckled as she left, then turned back to Christian. "I want to put an I team into Mahoney's group as we go through the process."

Christian nodded. "How do you want to put them in?"

"Mahoney says that Force hands all of the white people he comes across over to the Hibernians. Tell them to start getting ready. It will take them a few weeks of dieting in order to look like they've been living on the road, then we'll have them come up on Force from the south. He'll turn them over to Mahoney and they're in."

Christian nodded in approval. "Okay. I'll tell Mike to start getting them ready. Anything else?"

"Yep. Send Naomi to talk to the sheriffs in Cass and Bates counties and tell them we'll take that area if everyone still agrees. She can work out the boundary details with them."

"Okay."

Jim lifted his cup and drained it. "Now, let's go meet Dehmer and his Rangers."

5

Jeremy "JJ" Skaggs looked uneasily at the stone walls surrounding them as they maneuvered through the entry gate. "You've been here before, right?"

Dehmer nodded. "Yeah, a couple of times."

"Good. Just wanted to make sure it was possible to get back out."

Dehmer smiled. "Well, it has been so far."

Skaggs looked at him. "Very reassuring."

Dehmer chuckled. "These are good people. Real good. I told you about Mrs. Wyatt shooting that Guard captain in the head, didn't I?"

Skaggs looked back at the wall passing outside his window. "Yeah. Why do you think I'm worried?"

Dehmer chuckled again. "Well, just don't criticize her cooking."

"Don't worry, I won't."

Making the final turn and exiting the gate complex into the interior of the compound, Dehmer checked his mirrors to make sure the other three vehicles had followed him onto the approach drive and looked over at Skaggs. "Feel better now?"

Skaggs looked up the hill at the stone and timber house at the top. Several people were standing on a stone veranda watching them approach. "Yeah, well, there's still that whole being shot in the head thing."

Dehmer laughed as he pulled up to the side of the house and parked. "Just ask for seconds and you should be fine."

Putting the truck in park, he glanced to see the other trucks pulling in beside him, opened his door and stepped out. He looked at Skaggs. "Remember, ask for seconds."

Slamming the truck door, he looked up to see Jim, Christian and Kelly walking toward him and raised a hand in greeting. "Jim! Christian! Kelly!"

The three walked toward him, smiling, until they got within handshake distance.

Jim stuck out his hand. "Ken. Good to see you."

Dehmer nodded, accepting the hand. "You too, Jim."

He shook Christian's hand and nodded to Kelly, exchanging greetings with each of them, then turned toward Skaggs. "This is JJ Skaggs, who heads up our Ottawa company. JJ, this is Jim Wyatt, Kelly Wyatt and Christian Bell."

Skaggs shook both Jim and Christian's hands, then took off his hat and nodded to Kelly. "Pleased to meet you, ma'am."

Kelly smiled in return. "Thank you, JJ. Welcome to Stonemont."

She looked at both Dehmer and Skaggs "Are you guys hungry?"

Dehmer looked at Skaggs, who looked worried, then back at Kelly and shrugged. "Well, we've been on the road since morning and I imagine most of the men are ready for something, but we don't want to put you out. We carry road rations and can dig into them."

Kelly made a face and shook her head. "Nonsense. We've been expecting you. I'll get things together while Jim gets you settled in, and supper will be ready in about an hour."

Dehmer smiled. "Thank you, Mrs. Wyatt. That's nice of you. I know the men will appreciate it."

Kelly nodded. "Well, you'd better get used to it when you're at Stonemont, Ken. And you'd better start calling me Kelly. You make me feel old with all of this Mrs. Wyatt stuff."

Dehmer chuckled. "Okay, Kelly. Thank you."

Kelly looked at Skaggs sternly. "You too, JJ. You wouldn't want to insult me, would you?"

Skaggs shook his head seriously, still holding his hat at his side. "No ma'am, not a bit. I mean, no, Kelly. Thank you."

She giggled. "Good, then you guys get settled in and I'll see you in about an hour."

"Who's ready for some apple pie?" asked Kelly as she got up from the table.

JJ looked down at the faint traces of his second helpings of burnt ends, barbecue beans, corn bread and coleslaw and nodded somewhat feebly along with the rest of the Rangers at the table. "Yes ma'am. I'm gonna have to try."

Kelly laughed. "Very good. If you all wouldn't mind taking your plates over to the soaking tub but hanging onto your forks, Jenny will bring you out some new dessert plates and I'll bring out the pies."

Ken looked at Jim. "Do you always eat like this?"

Jim shook his head. "No, sometimes she really gets things going. She and Jenny kind of had to throw this together in a hurry."

Ken looked at Jim carefully, trying to figure out if he was kidding. "Well, for a quick throw-together, she sure put out a heck of a spread."

He looked around at his men. "I'd say these guys are now operating at about half-speed, so her cooking has done more to take them down than all of the outlaws in eastern Kansas."

Jim laughed. "There's nothing like being full of good food in a safe place to make a man relax. One of the oldest tricks in the book."

Ken chuckled. "So true." He took a sip of his sweet tea. "I hope we can get the rest of Kansas settled down like this someday."

"How are things shaping up, in your eyes?" asked Christian.

Ken leaned forward, placing his forearms on the table. "I'd say patchy."

"Patchy?"

Ken nodded. "We've got patches where everything is nice and calm, and we've got patches where it's not safe for anyone to go or live. The peaceful areas are the places where people have been able to fortify a location with enough people and firepower to keep the marauders from thinking they're an easy target - places like here and Riley. The areas in between are sketchy since the new state has started raiding."

Jim nodded. "Freelove and McGregor told us they've had some raids on their northern borders. Our scouts responded to a couple of them and said they were brutal."

He paused, looking at Ken closely. "Have you all been able to catch or identify any of the raiders?"

Ken looked at his hands on the table and shook his head. "Nope. We know they're new-staters because of the calling cards they leave, but we've always gotten there too late to catch or get an eyeball on any of them."

He looked back up at Jim. "It's a big area, and we don't have the manpower to cover it all or the intelligence capabilities to anticipate where they'll strike next."

Jim continued to watch Ken and nodded slowly. "That's a problem."

Ken nodded. "It's what I wanted to talk to you about."

"Who's ready?" asked Kelly, coming out of the kitchen door carrying two pies.

A chorus of "*I am*"s sounded from around the table and Jim leaned back in his chair, still looking at Ken. "Let's talk about it after pie."

They talked through coffee and both apple pies before most of the Rangers left for the cabins that had been prepared for them, leaving only Ken with Jim, Christian and Kelly.

The night had started to chill, but none of them wanted to go inside and leave the crisp fall air, so Jim got up to bring the coffee pot to the table. He filled Ken's cup first, then Christian's, then his own, then returned the pot to the warming stove and sat down.

He raised his cup to Kelly and smiled. "There's nothing better than hot coffee on a cool night, babe. You don't know what you're missing."

She smiled, snuggling deeper into her wool sweater. "I'm fine. I might make myself some tea later."

Jim nodded, took a sip, then set his cup down and looked at Ken. "You ready to talk about the rest?"

Ken took a sip of his own coffee, set the cup down and nodded, looking at Jim. "I wanted to ask you something, but I think I know what your answer is going to be so I didn't want to ask in front of the men."

Jim raised an eyebrow in question. "It sounds serious."

Ken leaned forward, resting his forearms on the table. "Like I said earlier, we're spread pretty thin. Besides the counties that have already joined the confederation, new counties are contacting us about joining, mainly for the protection they think belonging to the confederation can provide. Most are long on land and short on people, which means that they don't have many people to contribute to the effort."

Jim continued to watch Ken but said nothing.

"The extra area is going to spread us even thinner," Ken continued. "That makes it more dangerous for the men we do have, so we're trying to recruit more people."

He looked at Jim. "To cut to the chase, I came to ask you if you could provide some men to us or allow us to recruit here. You're stable because you are insulated from

45

the new state's attacks by the counties surrounding you. Contributing men or allowing us to recruit from you would help to further protect you by adding to the forces now providing that protection."

Jim took a slow sip of his coffee, set his cup down and leaned back in his chair. He had been expecting something like this.

Although the Rangers were competent and committed, they were comparatively small in number. The counties to the south and west had done well under the leadership of their sheriffs and with the support of their populations, but it was well accepted than none of them would be able to hold up under an assault by large, organized groups. This was exactly the situation he had discussed with Freelove and McGregor when they had asked him to join the confederation, and little had changed with the exception that the new state now posed an actual organized threat.

"I understand your situation," he said thoughtfully. "Christian and I have been discussing the need to build up our scouts as we assume responsibility for more territory."

Ken nodded. "By contributing to the Rangers, you would be helping to put more forces out on the front line, farther away from you. That would make you more secure here."

Jim shook his head. "What makes us secure here is our strength and the knowledge of our capabilities as exhibited in some of our previous actions, not the buffer of other counties. As we all know, and as you said, the counties around us have been raided. We have not been. In fact, it was our scouts that destroyed the recent new state raiding party some distance from us, making that area safer for those who live there and those who live around them."

Ken nodded again. "That's true. That was a streak of luck that you found out about that and were able to get some people up there it time. No doubt it saved a great many lives. That shows the importance of having stronger forces out in the areas where the raids are occurring."

Jim looked at Ken for a moment before responding, wondering whether he was purposefully trying to minimize Stonemont's involvement in the action or whether he really didn't understand.

"It didn't have anything to do with luck, Ken. Our foreknowledge of the raid was the result of our intelligence capabilities that are the result of our training programs and our scouts going to dangerous places to do dangerous things. Once we had the intelligence, other teams of our scouts went out and destroyed the units of the new state that were about to massacre a town. They saved the town and who knows how many others those dirtbags would have raided if they were still alive."

He leaned forward, placing his forearms on the table. "That operation was quite a distance from us, and we had no help from anyone else. Do you know why?"

Ken shook his head.

"Because no one had anybody they could send."

Ken looked at him for a minute, then at his coffee cup and nodded. "That's the problem," he said, then looked back up at Jim. "That's why we need your help."

Jim looked at him for a long moment, then at Christian who was watching closely, then back at Ken. "There's an old saying that you can't make a weak man stronger by making a strong man weaker. That's what this would be if we assigned some of our forces to you." He shook his head. "I won't do that."

Ken nodded slowly. It was the answer he had expected. "Then, how about allowing us to recruit from your people?"

Jim shook his head again. "Same thing. By allowing you to recruit here we would be weakening the pool of those going into the scouts. I'm sorry, but we can't do that."

Ken held Jim's gaze, not surprised at the answer but disappointed none the less. He didn't want to propose the next idea, but he had been instructed to and knew he had no choice.

"There has been talk among the confederation leadership of instituting a conscription of able-bodied men throughout the confederation," he said. "By willingly allowing us to recruit from Stonemont, you could avoid any forced conscription."

Jim felt himself grow cold at the thinly veiled threat. He could feel Christian looking at him but kept his attention on Ken. "That is, indeed, an interesting statement."

He pushed back his chair and rose to his feet. "I think this is a good time to turn in. There has been much said here for us to consider carefully, and a good night's sleep rarely hurts."

Ken and Christian both rose, Ken extending his hand. "Thank you for hearing me out."

Jim accepted the hand. "You're welcome. It's always important to know where everyone stands."

Ken nodded. "Well, thank you."

He started to turn away, then turned back. "I want you to know that the message I brought was not my own. I was instructed to bring it by the confederation council." He paused before continuing. "I don't necessarily agree with it."

Jim nodded. "I suspected as much, but thank you for telling me. Bring your men over for breakfast, then we can talk again privately. I'll have a message for you to take back with you."

Ken nodded, started to say something, then stopped and turned to walk toward the cabins.

Jim watched him walk away into the darkness, picked his cup up and drained it, then turned to Christian. "Let's go to my study. We have some things to talk about."

6

Morning brought the first frost of the year and breakfast was a grab-what-you-can affair as the Les Chenes group and Aaron's team prepared to leave. Vapor-breath seemed to accentuate the excitement as the column formed up in the commons and the clear, crisp air seemed to amplify the shouts and laughter of both those about to depart and those assisting them.

Mike stood with Tracy and his family, apart from the rest of the activity, as they talked quietly and said their goodbyes. The reunion had been a blessing to all of them, one that each felt deeply, and the approaching moment of separation seemed almost surreal in its immediacy, causing each to fumble in self-conscious superficiality and semi-silence as they fought to find the words that would adequately express their deepest feelings in the short time remaining.

The Las Chenes troops shook the hands and returned the best wishes of the Stonemont residents, and Aaron's scouts fought to contain their excitement for the coming adventure, their attention split between those they were saying goodbye to and their eagerness to be underway.

Finally, sensing that further delay would allow the height of emotion to dwindle into anticlimactic confusion, Jim stepped off the veranda and walked to where Augustus stood with the rest of the Carpenters and said a few words to Augustus.

Augustus replied, took a step back and saluted.

Jim returned the salute.

Augustus then turned abruptly to Mike, presenting a crisp salute to his youngest son.

Momentarily confused, Mike fought to maintain his composure, brought himself to rigid attention and returned the salute.

Snapping his right arm to his side, Augustus stepped toward Mike, took him in his arms and held him while they spoke quietly to each other for over a minute.

Finally releasing his son, Augustus signaled for the Les Chenes troops to mount up, gave a final nod and word to Jim, Christian, Kelly and the Garners, then walked to his own vehicle.

The sound of starting engines filled the commons, then settled into a steady rumble as the lead truck headed toward the main gate. The others followed and Jim watched as the column disappeared into the gate complex.

Christian looked at him. "You want me to go get Ken?"

Jim looked at the rising sun and shook his head. "Let's let Mike settle down a bit. I want him there, and you can tell him to invite his brother if he wants to."

He cocked his head toward the house. "Let's have breakfast and talk to Ken afterward."

Ken followed Kelly down the hallway to the study and stopped as he entered the large room. A fire blazed in the large fireplace on the opposite side of the room, in front of which a horseshoe of couches was arranged around a large, low table. Jim sat on the couch to the left and Christian and Mike shared the couch on the right.

Seeing Ken enter, Jim rose from his couch. "Come in, Ken. We were just talking about you." He gestured toward the vacant middle couch. "Have a seat. Can I get you a cup of coffee?"

Ken nodded. "Thanks."

Ken sat and looked around the room as Jim went to the sideboard to pour a new mug of coffee. The room was large, but with a feeling of warmth. The high ceilings were timbered, as was the framing of the rest of the room, and expansive paned windows on the two side walls made him feel like he could see the whole world around him. More windows bracketed the massive stone fireplace in front of him and behind him were floor-to-ceiling shelves of books.

"Here you go," said Jim, setting the cup in front of him. "Did you sleep well?"

Ken nodded. "I did. Thank you. My men and I appreciate your hospitality."

Jim smiled as he sat back down on the couch. "Good. I hope you'll come back often. We like to take good care of friends."

He took a sip of his coffee and leaned back. "Christian and I have been talking about the confederation's request for men. You understand why we can't comply, don't you?"

Ken nodded. "I do. As I said, it was not my idea. I was just delivering a message."

Jim nodded. "I understand. You did the job you were asked to do. The Rangers and the confederation will be well served by your leadership."

Ken took a sip of his coffee but remained silent, not yet sure of the direction the conversation would be taking.

"Still," said Jim, leaning forward, "that leaves the problem of vast areas remaining unprotected from the rising new state, not to mention other assorted marauders."

Ken nodded. "Yes, it does."

Jim looked at Ken closely. "I want to explain my reason to you so that you'll understand and be able to explain it to the confederation council."

Again, Ken nodded without saying anything.

"It took a lot to secure and build up Stonemont and the area we now hold as our autonomous area," continued Jim. "It started as our home, gradually grew into a community and finally a collection of communities operating under our protection and authority. The key has been the combined efforts of many good people working within the framework of shared values."

Ken nodded a third time. "You've done a remarkable job."

Jim nodded in return. "Thank you. The key has been central leadership. While I seek and consider the advice of those around me, I make the final decisions according to what I think is in the best interests of those who depend on those decisions for their safety and welfare. I don't put things up for a vote and I don't put myself under anyone else's authority. That has allowed us to make the progress we have instead of wasting time dealing with the politics of other groups."

He picked up his coffee mug and took a sip before setting it back down and continuing. "The confederation wants us to provide forces for the protection of people and areas for which we currently have no responsibility, over which we have no authority, and which does nothing to support us. If you remember your history, you'll remember that the former United States assumed the role of protector all over the world for those who could not protect themselves, and in doing so sacrificed a great many of its own citizens and resources."

He shook his head. "Assuming responsibility for things we don't control is a recipe for disaster, both for us and for relationships within the confederation."

He paused, looking at Ken. "If the confederation can think of another way, I'll be happy to listen."

Ken shrugged. "I can't think of another way, but I'll tell them."

Jim stood up. "Well, you tell them what I said and maybe they can think of another way. Until then, you and your men are welcome here anytime and we hope to see you again soon."

Ken rose, feeling that there was a hidden message somewhere in Jim's words that he wasn't quite able to see. He extended his hand. "Thank you, Jim. I'll pass your message back. And thank you again for your hospitality."

Jim took his hand. "It's always good to see you, Ken."

He turned to Mike. "Mike, would you see Ken out? I want to talk to Christian for a minute."

Mike nodded and walked Ken out of the study.

Jim watched them leave, then turned to Christian. "Tell me what you're thinking."

Christian looked at Jim, then out the window, thinking, then back at Jim. "I think you're playing chess, but I don't see the next move."

"That's because the next move is theirs."

Christian looked at his uncle closely. "What do you think it will be? Or should I say what do you *want* it to be?"

Jim looked out the window for a moment, then shrugged. "We will see. Right now, I'm going to take Kelly out for a ride."

He started to walk toward the door, then stopped and turned around. "Tell Mike to increase recruiting as much as he can, including the outlying areas we haven't really tapped yet. I want as many scouts as we can get in the field as fast as we can get them."

Christian nodded. "Will do."

Kelly gave her horse a cluck and reined it alongside Jim's, shaking her head to get her hair out of her face. She looked over at him. "So, what brought this on?"

Jim shrugged. "It's a beautiful day and it's been a while since we've been out. We might not get many more days like this before winter hits."

She smiled. "You're right. I'm already getting that winter feeling."

He chuckled. "Remember when we lived in the 'burbs and you'd buy all those pumpkins, corn stalks and hay bales to make it look like we lived in the country?"

She laughed. "I liked it." She gave him a sideways glance. "I think you did too."

He smiled and nodded. "Yeah, I did."

"So, are we going anywhere in particular or just horsing around?"

He laughed. "Well, we can horse around if you want to, but there's something I want to show you first."

Her eyes twinkled. "Is it better than horsing around?"

He shrugged. "That's hard to say. I guess it depends on the moment."

"Okay. Show me first and then we can horse around. Then I'll tell you which was better."

He laughed. "Okay. Give her a kick. We've got a ways to go."

They descended into the valley and let the horses out to lope across the fields. The green of summer had given way to the browns and beiges of autumn, and they soon reached the trail that led up to the top of the hill he had been on two days before.

As with the fields, the green of the trees had changed to their fall colors, and they soon found themselves surrounded by the yellows and oranges of the canopy they now rode under, the sun dappling the trail and making the leaves seem to glow around them.

"This reminds me of that time we rode through Dogwood Canyon," said Kelly. "Remember?"

He smiled. "I remember."

"I wonder how things are down there?"

Jim thought about that time, and the many other times they had spent around Table Rock Lake in southern Missouri. Big Cedar Lodge had been their go-to home-away-from-home when they wanted to get away and Silver Dollar City had become their favorite destination as the kids got older. They had even had dreams of the children going to College of the Ozarks. "Yeah, I wonder. Maybe I'll have the Ozark teams go through there and see."

She looked over at him. "Do you ever think about those times?"

He shook his head. "No. We've been a bit busy."

He looked at her. "Do you?"

"Sometimes. Those were good times."

He nodded. "Yes, they were."

They ascended the hill on the switchback trail, enjoying the vibrant colors, the earthy smell and the soft breeze that rustled the leaves above them. They rode in comfortable silence, enjoying the time together alone and hearing only the hoof falls on the soft loam of the trail, the creaking of saddle leather and an occasional blow from one of the horses.

Finally reaching the crest, they exited the trees into the park-like setting of the hilltop and stopped. Beyond them spread the miles of rolling lowland to the south and west.

Kelly gasped. "Oh my gosh! I never knew this was here! What an amazing view!"

Jim dismounted and moved around her horse, extending his hand up to her. "Let's get down for a minute."

Taking his hand, she dismounted, and they stood together looking out over the valley. Cattle and buffalo dotted the land beneath them and two eagles floated above the valley floor, though lower than where they stood.

"It's breathtaking," she said.

He nodded. "Remember when we used to talk about building a cabin somewhere like this?"

She nodded, smiling. "Those were nice dreams."

He walked several feet away, turned toward her and held his arms out. "I thought we'd put the front door right here, looking out over the valley."

She laughed. "You're funny."

He shrugged. "Well, I sure don't want it facing the trees."

She looked at him quizzically. "Are you serious? You want to build a cabin here?"

He shook his head. "A house. *Our* new house."

Her eyes got wide. "Really? Why?"

He turned back to look across the valley. "We built Stonemont as our private home and getaway. It's become the center of a thriving and bustling community, bringing us great rewards but little of the privacy we built it to provide. It doesn't feel like our home anymore. It feels like a headquarters. Just as I want the others to build their own places, I want to build us a new home where we can enjoy the privacy a family needs."

He walked back over to her, turning again to look out over the valley and put his arm around her shoulders. "So, what do you think? The front door right there?"

She shook her head slowly. "I don't know what to think." She looked up at him. "Can we make it look like Top of the Rock?"

He smiled and shrugged. "I don't see why not."

7

Malcolm Coates strode across the expansive marble floor under the rotunda, enjoying the echoes of his heel strikes in the cavernous space and the effect he knew it had on the timid souls who were allowed to work in the Capitol. He caught two such munchkins looking at him disapprovingly until he locked his eyes on them, at which point they scurried away. He thought about having a little fun with them, but decided to get first things out of the way first. The general probably thought he was dead, and now was the time for the surprise.

He mounted the steps to the main floor, taking them lightly for a man his size, and would have smiled at the thought of the approaching meeting if he was a man given to smiling, but he wasn't and he didn't.

Reaching the main floor, he walked around the railed rotunda walkway, then down a short hallway to a door with a frosted glass window on which was written Gen. Herndon Briggs, Commanding General, Army of New Kansas.

He smirked and opened the door to see a thin young man in an ill-fitting uniform behind a desk.

The young man looked up, his eyes widening at the sight of Coates, and he half-rose out of his seat as if unsure of whether to stand or not. "Uh, I'm sorry, may I help you?"

Coates looked at him as he passed. "You're sorry, alright. Sit down."

Walking to an inner door, he turned the knob and pushed it open to see General Briggs seated behind a large desk writing on a yellow legal pad.

Briggs looked up, a mixture of surprise and irritation showing on his face. "Who are you?" he demanded.

Coates walked to a chair in front of Briggs' desk and sat down without being asked. "I'm Malcom Coates."

Recognition came slowly to Briggs. He remembered the one they had called Stark's hammer after Johnny had been killed. He set his pen aside. "I thought you were dead."

"Not yet."

Briggs looked at the man closely, trying to decipher the cold black eyes. "And Stark?"

"Dead."

"How?"

"Killed by one of his own men."

Briggs leaned back in his chair, trying not to show his shock. "Why?"

Coates shrugged. "I guess he didn't like him."

Briggs took a moment to digest that. "And the rest?"

"Dead."

Briggs stared at Coates. "All of them?"

"All of them."

The two men stared at each other in silence before Coates spoke again.

"I'm taking over the army."

The words, and the flat tone with which they were spoken, sent a sudden chill through Briggs and he thought about the pistol in his desk drawer. He couldn't remember whether the drawer was locked, and he suddenly felt himself sweating.

"You can keep being the General in everyone else's eyes," Coates continued, "but you're soft, and your so-called army is nothing more than a bunch of mis-fits who can't make it on their own. That's why that bunch got slaughtered. And that's why I killed Stark."

He saw the flash of shock in Briggs' eyes.

"That's right. I killed him. Just like I'm going to kill you in a minute if you don't come on board right now."

Briggs suddenly felt sick to his stomach, and he pressed the palms of his hands against the desktop to give himself a sense of stability. "Captain Jensen!" he called to the young man in the front office.

Jensen's head appeared in the doorway. "Yes, General?"

Briggs fought to keep his voice even. "Would you ask Colonel Bates to come in here, please?"

Jensen's head disappeared and a muffled "Yessir" could be heard from the front office.

Coates smiled. "So, Bates is your second in command? Good. When he gets here you can tell him that I will be assuming operational control of the army."

He drew a black pistol from inside his jacket and held it casually in his lap. "If you don't, I'll kill him - right after I kill you."

Briggs could feel sweat breaking out on his upper lip and at his temples. The thought that someone could walk into his office and just take over the army by threat of personal force against him was more than he could process, and the man was giving him no time. "You can't just take over an army like that."

Coates smiled again. "One more statement like that, even one more thought like that, and I'll be dealing with Bates directly."

Briggs felt his head go from hot to cold and he recognized the adrenalin rush that was making him start to shake.

Coates watched him.

"This should be the easiest decision you've made in your life, General, but you don't have long to make it.

Think carefully about what two things could happen in the next few minutes."

Briggs' mouth was dry, and he tried to swallow but couldn't. He stared into Coates' eyes and was hit with the realization that wearing a uniform for thirty years in an office had not prepared him for a threat of actual personal violence. His mind spun without being able to find a direction, and, as if through a thick filter, he heard footsteps and Bates' voice ask, "You asked for me, General?"

Briggs struggled to break the hold Coates' eyes had on him and nodded stiffly. "Yes, Colonel."

He looked back at Coates. "I wanted to let you know that Major Coates has been promoted to the rank of Brigadier General and will assume operational control of the army as of now."

A fleeting look of surprise crossed Bates' face before he caught himself. "Very good, sir."

He turned to Coates. "Congratulations, General."

Coates' smile didn't reach his eyes. "Thank you, Colonel."

He stood up, sliding the pistol back into his jacket so that Bates couldn't see it and looked back at Briggs. "I'll begin the pacification program we discussed immediately, General. I'm not sure when or how often I'll be able to check in for a while, so maybe I should just come past your house whenever I need to."

Briggs felt the cold grip of the threat and rose to his feet, his legs weak. "That's not necessary, General. Just touch base with me here when you can. I'm sure you don't need my direction."

Coates' smile got bigger. "It's no problem, General. I know where you live, and I always enjoy seeing your wife and daughters. I'll check in with you whenever I need to."

He turned and nodded at Bates. "Colonel."

Bates watched Coates leave, then looked at Briggs, who seemed shaken. "Are you alright, General?"

Briggs continued to look at the empty doorway for a moment, then looked down at the legal pad on his desk. His last note to himself had been to solidify Army leadership.

He looked up at Bates. "Yes, Colonel. Thank you." He began gathering papers from his desk and placing them in a leather portfolio. His hands were shaking slightly. "I'll be working at home for the rest of the day."

Bates watched as Briggs zipped up the case and put on his overcoat. "Very good, General. I'll send a messenger if anything important comes up."

Briggs seemed not to hear him as he walked out the door.

Coates walked out of the South doors of the capital and started down the steps. Briggs had been easier than he had thought he'd be, but maybe he shouldn't have been surprised - those who got their power from behind a desk often crumbled when confronted by an imminent threat of personal violence. No longer insulated by layers of minions and volumes of policies and regulations, they were often stunned into paralysis by their sudden understanding of their aloneness in a world of personal physical threat. He had seen that Briggs had fully understood his threat against his wife and daughters and figured he had put enough nails in that coffin - at least for now.

He descended the steps, walked down the south walkway and got into his jeep. It had been stripped of all of the electronics it had come with and retrofitted with an old Chevy 327 engine with compatible transmission, just like his first car had had. Pulling away from the curb, he thought about stopping by The Weed, but decided against it and headed out to the zoo.

The city was declining even from the initial pus hole it had become after the collapse. Lack of electricity, gas and running water had roughened the people from their previous semi-refinement to the point where they reminded him of refugees he had seen in eastern Europe and the city itself was falling apart. Potholes pocked every street, grass and weeds grew up through every sidewalk and the buildings themselves seemed to be crumbling more each day. It seemed like there was dust everywhere.

The dwindling population had grown more furtive, more feral and more volatile with each passing month and he wondered how much longer the leadership of New Kansas could keep up the facade of a functional government.

He let his mind wander back to his army days. He had resented the discipline that he felt suppressed his true talents, but he had stayed within the lines enough to stay out of the brig, and he had learned a lot - a lot that he was now ready to use for his own purposes. He chuckled to himself. He supposed he should be grateful to Uncle Sam for that.

He thought about driving through town to see the progressive decay of the neighborhoods, a decay that somehow made him feel good witnessing it, but headed toward the highway instead, in order to talk to the men while he was still in the proper mood.

Taking the ramp onto I-70, he headed north, then took the westbound loop around the north of Topeka, finally exiting onto Gage Boulevard and heading south toward the zoo.

The zoo had been Stark's idea, a stupid idea he was about the rectify. He had enjoyed eating the animals, not because they were good, because they weren't, but because of the idea of eating lions, elephants, bear and other predators. He had heard someone say that if you ate another predator, it gave you greater strength. He didn't know if that was true or not, but he knew it was true that he had eaten a lion, an elephant, and a bear.

He turned right onto SW 6th Avenue, then left onto Zoo Parkway which led into Gage Park and followed it to where it turned into Munn Memorial Drive encircling the encampment where hundreds of tents of various designs and colors filled the area. Pulling up to the curb next to the restrooms, he shut off the jeep, got out and strode to the command tent where he found Captain Jorge Rodriguez sitting at a table with several lieutenants.

He walked to within ten feet of Rodriguez and stopped. "Stand up."

Rodriguez's eyes narrowed and he rose smoothly to his feet, consciously expanding his chest and biceps as he smiled. The time had been coming for a while and he would use it to impress his subordinates while he made his play for command. "What's up, Coates?"

Coates brought up the gun in his hand and pulled the trigger. A small dot appeared on Rodriguez's forehead and blood, brain tissue and bone fragments sprayed the two lieutenants behind him. Rodriguez's body remained standing for a moment, then collapsed as the nervous system stopped sending signals to the muscles.

Coates looked at the lieutenants. "He questioned an order of mine once and showed disrespect just now. I am now General Coates, in command of the army. You are all now captains. Have your men ready to leave at daybreak."

8

Jim carried his boots and gun belt to the door and turned around. It was still too dark to see her clearly, but the soft sounds of Kelly's breathing brought a smile to his face, and he stood there for a moment listening. Satisfied that his rising hadn't awakened her, he opened the bedroom door, walked down the hallway and descended the stairs to the kitchen.

Navigating by the faint light coming through the windows, he hung his gun belt over the back of a chair and sat down to pull on his boots, noticing that it felt chillier than usual. Getting back to his feet, he walked to the wood stove and opened the door to the fire box, stirred up the banked coals from the previous night and added a few sticks of wood to get a flame going. Satisfied that the flames had taken hold, he added a few more sticks, shut the door of the fire box and put the large enamel percolating coffee pot on the cooktop.

Walking to the stone fireplace, he took a lighter out of his pocket and squatted to light the feathered slice of fatwood in the pre-laid stack of tinder and split wood. The fatwood caught immediately and sent the first flame into the tinder, which caught and sent larger flames to lick the split sticks and logs above it.

He stayed there for a moment, watching the fire establish itself, then rose and walked to look out the window. He smiled. It was snowing.

He watched as the flakes floated down in the moonlight, the promise of sunrise still a few minutes away, and thought about how snow made people happy. It always had, and he wondered, as he always had, whether that was simply because of its beauty or the feeling of shared experience it gave people. Probably a bit of both.

He looked across the commons and judged that the snow had started recently, having only laid a first dusting on the ground and flat surfaces. The kids would be excited, and he thought about whether he should let them stay home from school to enjoy it.

He stayed there for several minutes, just watching the snow, until he heard the water bubbling in the coffee pot. Taking his pine tree mug off the shelf, he filled it with hot water, then put a spoonful of Folgers instant into it. He stirred for a few seconds before rinsing the spoon and placing it aside.

Taking a sip to assure himself of the right taste, he set the mug on the counter, poured a medium measure of grounds into the basket of the coffee pot and placed it back on the grate to percolate.

The scout teams had left for southern Missouri three days before and things had started to settle down after the excitement of their departure. The coming of winter and the promise of the holidays had everyone shifting mental gears as they downshifted from the business of summer and the harvest to a mindset of the comparative rest and rejuvenation of winter. Just as nature needed the dormancy of winter to rest and prepare itself for the explosive rebirth of spring, so too did people, and the new world allowed that, even dictated it, in a way the old world had not.

He returned to the window to watch the snow, which seemed to have picked up in only the last few minutes, a smooth blanket now covering the commons. A light came on in Christian and Naomi's cabin.

He took another sip of his coffee, thinking about the first snow after the collapse. Then, it had been a serious threat to the many who were not prepared to enter the winter months without electricity. Now, the community they had built provided the safety that made snow beautiful again.

He wondered if there were any still out in the world trying to make it on their own without joining a community and he supposed there had to be. People came in all flavors.

The sound of the percolator reminded him of his grandparents' farmhouse which always smelled of coffee and whatever was cooking for the next meal - but always coffee.

He remembered his grandfather's large, calloused hands and quiet ways - so gentle to those he loved, yet so hard and steady when those he loved were threatened. He looked at the table and imagined his grandfather and father sitting there talking and drinking coffee. They both would have done very well in this new world, and he felt a sudden flash of solidarity with them.

"What are you looking at?"

He turned to see Kelly standing in the doorway wearing her favorite faded sweatshirt and fleece lounge pants. He smiled. "I was just thinking about my dad and granddad." He nodded toward the table. "I could almost see them sitting there drinking coffee."

She glanced at the table. "I wish I could have known them."

He nodded. "You would have liked them. My uncle, too. And they would have liked you."

She finger-combed her hair back as she walked toward him, looking again at the table. "Do you miss them?"

He thought for a moment while he took another sip. "It's been so long that I wouldn't say I miss them. I wish they were here, though."

She stopped in front of him and looked up at him, smiling. "Were they like you?"

He chuckled. "It's probably more appropriate to say that I'm like them."

She nodded. "Then I really wish I could have known them." She smiled. "Would you like an omelet?"

"Sure."

"What do you want in it?"

"Whatever you put in it."

"Bacon, sausage, onion, mushrooms, basil, rosemary, cilantro, sage, parsley and cheese?"

He cocked an eyebrow. "No strawberries?"

"It's November."

"Well, okay."

"It's snowing!"

She moved around him excitedly to get a better look out the window. "The kids will be ecstatic! Should we let them stay home from school?"

He turned back around to look out the window with her and nodded. "I was thinking that."

"Maybe we should make the first day of snow a school holiday every year."

He smiled and shrugged. "Sounds like a good idea. Should we let them sleep in or wake them up to tell them they don't have to wake up to go to school?"

"Let's wake them up after we finish eating. Will you make them pancakes? They'd love that."

He chuckled. "You bet."

He looked out the window and saw that a light in Mike and Tracy's cabin had come on. "What have you got going on today?"

"Nothing special. I think I'll just stay around the house and hang out with the kids. How about you?"

He turned back toward her. "I've got to meet with Christian and Mike for a while this morning, but after that I'm with you all."

She smiled as she walked toward the pantry to gather the ingredients she needed. "Good."

They ate their omelets, then woke and made pancakes for the kids. The snow had gained strength around daybreak, then settled back into the kind of steady fall that could last all day and a blanket of white now lay on everything outside.

"Can we go sledding?" asked Brody as he carried his plate to the sink.

Jim chuckled. "Well, I guess we could if we had sleds, buddy."

Kelly brought her plate and the empty pancake platter to the sink and turned on the faucet. "I'm sure we can find some things for you guys to slide down a hill on. We'll go look after we clean up and you all get dressed."

"Why not sleds?" asked Brody.

Kelly smiled. "Because we don't have any sleds, honey."

"Yes, we do."

She looked at him with amusement. "We do? Where?"

"Remember last year when the scouts brought in that trailer filled with winter stuff? It had a bunch of saucers and sleds that dad said we could use to pull stuff around on."

She looked at Jim. "I remember that. Do you have any idea where they are?"

Jim shook his head. "Nope, but I bet you have it in your inventory folders."

She looked back at Brody and smiled. "You have an amazing memory, buddy. You want to go try to find them after we get cleaned up?"

Brody smiled and gave a self-satisfied nod. "Yep!"

It took them a little over an hour after they got dressed to find the notation for the sleds, then locate the trailer in which they were stored.

Opening the rear doors, Aedan and Brody climbed into the trailer and began working their way over crates of

Christmas lights, fake Christmas trees and ornaments. About halfway back, Brody yelled, "I found them!"

Jim looked up into the trailer. "How many are there?"

"About a million!"

Jim chuckled. "A million?"

"Well ... about a hundred. Maybe more!"

"How many should we get out?" called Aedan.

Jim turned to Kelly. "How many kids are there in town?"

She thought for a moment and shrugged. "Several hundred."

"Get 'em all out!" Jim yelled.

Aedan's head popped up from behind a box, an inquisitive look on his face. "*All* of them?"

Jim nodded with a smile. "All of them. I'll be back in a few minutes after I hook a trailer up to the Excursion."

The tires of the Excursion made a final crunch in the snow as they stopped on the crest of the hill overlooking Jamestown. Jim put it in park and opened his door. "Alright, let's get them unloaded."

"What are we going to do with all of them?" asked Morgan as she got out, walking back to meet her dad at the trailer.

Jim smiled as he dropped the rear ramp of the trailer. "We're going to deliver them to the kids in town."

She scrunched her face in question. "Deliver them? How?"

He chuckled. "Everybody grab a couple of sleds and follow me. I'll show you."

They each picked two sleds out of the trailer and followed him to the top of the hill where they stopped, looking down at the town.

Jim put a sled on the ground, pointed it downhill and gave it a push with his foot. The sled started slowly at first, then picked up speed as the incline increased and shot down the hill.

Jim repeated the process with the second sled and turned toward the others, smiling. "Go ahead. We've got a lot of sleds to deliver!"

Two by two, they sent their sleds down the hill toward the town, each returning to the trailer to get more. After several rounds, the hillside was littered with brightly colored sleds, some making it all the way down and some getting stuck on the way. A young boy walking with his parents looked up to see the approaching sleds and stopped. Looking up at his parents, who nodded, he broke into a full run toward the hill.

"It looks like he's going for that red one," smiled Kelly.

"Here comes another one!" said Brody, seeing another boy running up the hill.

"And a girl!" yelled Morgan, happy to see one of her own now going after a prize.

Aedan walked up with an armload of sleds. "It looks like the word's getting out."

Jim nodded, seeing more children breaking from their school-ward walk to claim a prize of their own. He turned to his son. "How many more do we have?"

Aedan shrugged. "A bunch."

Jim turned back to look down the hill and smiled. "Good. Send 'em all down."

"Should I go down and tell them there's no school today?" asked Kelly.

Jim shrugged. "Sure, if you want to. I think they're figuring it out, though."

"I'd better go tell the parents and teachers," said Kelly, laughing. "That way, it's a holiday instead of an insurrection."

"Can we go down on a sled together, mom?" asked Morgan excitedly.

Kelly shook her head. "I'll ride down with dad. You kids finish sending the rest of the sleds down and then you can sled down yourselves."

"Pleeeeaase?" pleaded Morgan, planting herself in front of her mother.

Kelly looked at Jim, who was chuckling, then back at her daughter. "Don't you want to just go down with your brothers, sweetie?"

Morgan shook her head emphatically. "No, I want to go down with *you*."

"But I'll just slow you down," Kelly attempted to reason. "You'll go a lot faster if I'm not on the sled with you."

Morgan narrowed her eyes. "I don't want to go fast. I want to go with *you*."

She gave an impish smile. "Are you scared?"

Kelly again looked at Jim, who was watching with a widening smile. "But dad wants me to drive down with him, don't you, honey?"

Jim shook his head, his smile growing even bigger. "That's okay, babe. You go with Morgan. Have a good time. I'll see you at the bottom of the hill."

Kelly shot him a mock glare. "Maybe you should come *with* us."

Jim laughed. "Can't. Gotta drive the truck down."

Kelly narrowed her eyes at him for second before turning back to Morgan. "Okay, honey. Apparently, dad doesn't care if mom breaks her neck."

Morgan smiled and ran to get the purple sled she had picked for herself. "You're not going to break your neck. *Come on*!"

Jim laughed as Kelly shot him a parting scowl, then watched the two as they walked toward the top of the grade and sit on the sled.

"Are you ready?" Aedan yelled.

"Ready!" Morgan yelled as Brody gave a thumbs up.

"Okay, go!"

Aedan and Brody took running starts, throwing themselves onto the sleds as the sleds hit the ground, while Morgan and Kelly pushed themselves forward with their hands.

Jim watched as both boys shot down the hill, followed by their sister and mother, then turned back to the truck and got in. The engine roared to life, and he circled back to take the road into Jamestown.

The snow had slowed a bit, but he drove slowly, enjoying the beauty of the scene and the leisure to appreciate it.

He thought about the teams headed south toward the Ozarks and South Carolina, as well as the developing situations closer to home, but he pushed those thoughts from his mind. There was nothing he could do about them that he hadn't already done, and today was a day for family. Being with them was the only thing that was important today.

He drove for several minutes, taking note of the snow-covered fields and pastures of livestock huddled in their herds against the weather, then came around the final bend in the road that became South Street as it entered town.

The town looked like a Christmas card with its snow-cover, and the people walking along and across the streets gave it the feel of an old movie. A dog ran barking toward the hill, and he saw dozens of people lined up at the bottom watching their children going through the age-old tradition of trudging sleds uphill and riding them down, over and over again.

He swung the Excursion onto a newly graded side street at the bottom of the hill in order to keep the trailer out of the way of other traffic, shut it off and got out.

The noise of the children's shrieks of joy brought back memories of his own childhood and he stood there for a

72

moment to watch the semi-controlled mayhem on the hill above him. The bright colors of the sleds added a vibrancy to the scene that the mostly natural colored clothing didn't provide, and he realized once again how much the collapse had changed the accepted normalcy of life.

Movement coming toward him caught his attention and he watched Kelly and Morgan approach, both covered with snow.

"You two look like you came down without a sled!" he laughed.

"Dad, it was awesome!" squealed Morgan. "We kept crashing!"

He laughed again "You look like it!"

"How about you?" he asked, grinning at Kelly. "Did you leave any snow on the hill?"

"Maybe a little," Kelly grumbled, brushing snow off her jacket and snow pants. "I have snow in places I don't want to say out loud."

"Jim?"

Jim turned to see Mike standing several feet away, a serious look on his face. He looked at his chief of scouts. "What is it?"

Mike held a folded piece of paper out to him. "Two scouts are missing."

Jim looked at Mike for another second before reaching out for the paper. Unfolding it, he read the message it contained.

He looked back up at Mike. "How long?"

Mike shrugged. "The last time she was seen was right after dinner yesterday. She had today off, so nobody knew anything until one of her team went past her place about a half hour ago. The same with him."

Jim looked back at the letter again, shaking his head, then looked to the northeast and the city.

9

Ragan placed another stick on the small fire and looked over at the man snoring gently on the ground beside it.

Kyle was still a boy, really, - big on the outside but impetuous on the inside, and his decision to follow her still angered her as it might have put them both in more danger than had already existed. Still, she understood. She had also done something she wasn't supposed to.

She stared into the fire, a huge no-no for scouts, but indulged herself because of her confidence that she would be able to hear any movement in the cave before seeing it anyway and let her thoughts drift back to Stonemont.

Christian had said no to her plan, and he had said it emphatically - just as Mike had said he would. She had jumped chain and approached Jim directly, hoping to be able to sell her idea to him, but he had also said no - more gently, but even more emphatically.

Their refusal had disappointed her, if not surprised her, and she had thought about it hard for several days before coming to her decision.

She understood that their refusal came from their concern for her, but her own feeling of loyalty to Stonemont, a feeling she had never really expressed to anyone or fully understood herself, drove her to her decision to go against their wishes. If her idea worked, it could help ensure the safety of Stonemont, even if irreparably damaging her own reputation and relationship with those she now cared about more than any others in the world.

Kyle stirred and muttered something in his sleep that she couldn't make out, then settled back down.

She looked at him, thinking. It had been a week since she had left, having excused herself from the group eating dinner at the training hall with the excuse of a headache, then waiting until two hours after sunset to start off. The home guard prided itself on keeping their patrols irregular, but her experience had allowed her to slip through their web and she was into Missouri by the time the snow started falling.

She might not have seen him if it hadn't been for the white background of the snow, but, checking her back trail after sunrise, she had seen him moving in the woods about a hundred yards behind her. She hadn't recognized him at first, as he, like her, had changed from his uniform into civies, and her first impulse had been to try to lose him.

He had stuck with her though, neither falling farther behind nor closing on her, and she eventually circled around a rock outcropping to attempt an ambush. She had been just about to make her jump when she recognized him.

She put another stick on the fire and moved some coals to the side. Pouring some water into the small steel pot she had brought with her, she placed the pot on the coals to boil.

She looked at Kyle again and wondered if she should just leave him here. Maybe he'd go back to Stonemont. She thought about that but knew he wouldn't. He had refused to go back when she caught him following her and she knew he would again.

She reached into the small pack beside her and took out a Knorr Parmesan Fettuccine Side which she tore open and poured into the now-simmering water. They had gone without eating since arriving at the cave two days before in order to look a bit more haggard, but she had decided that it was time to go to the next step in her plan and they would need some energy.

Reaching back into the pack, she took out two packets of tuna which she opened, scooping the contents into the pot with a spoon. Placing a lid on the pot, she looked over to see Kyle watching her.

"We finally get to eat?" he asked, his eyes fixed on hers.

She nodded. "Today's the day."

She looked at the fire for a moment, then back at Kyle. "I need you to listen to me. I need to do this alone. It will be more dangerous for me if you're with me."

He stared at her; his face impassive. "Why?"

"Because I can play the scared victim role easier if I'm alone. Men respond to that. If you're with me, it adds a whole different dynamic. Then, I'm part of a pair. They can use us against each other. They can threaten me to get to you and threaten you to get to me. It makes both of us weaker - not stronger."

Kyle rolled up into a sitting position. "But you'd be all alone. At least with me you would have somebody to have your back."

She shook her head. "You wouldn't have my back. Not because you wouldn't try, but because you couldn't."

She looked up the dark tunnel of the limestone cave toward the entrance that was just now beginning to show the lighter grey of dawn. "We'd be going into an area controlled by a large, well-armed and organized group, and eventually taken prisoner. You couldn't stand against that. *We* couldn't stand against that."

She looked at him closely, trying to make her voice convey the seriousness of the situation as well as her conviction. "The best way for me to survive and do what I need to do is to go in alone. You have to trust me on this."

He remained silent for a minute, staring at her and willing her to change her mind. He knew she was right. He had always known that he would not be any real help once they entered the city. His reason for following her had mainly been to be with her on the way and try to change her mind.

"There has to be another way," he said.

She shook her head again. "None that we can be sure of."

She glanced at the fire, then looked back at him. "Mahoney wants to move his people out of the city. Jim is thinking about letting them move into the area east of us, but he doesn't know how much he can trust them. We know that Force turns everyone who's not like him over to the Irish, which means Mahoney. I walk into Force's area alone. He turns me over to Mahoney, thereby inserting me into the Irish without there being any connection to Stonemont. I stay with the Irish long enough to know what they're about, then head back out to Stonemont to tell Jim."

Kyle took a deep breath and let it out. "What if Force's people just catch you and kill you?" He paused before continuing in a quieter voice. "They could do other stuff too, you know."

She gave a small smile at his obvious concern. "They're not going to. We know enough about Force to know that."

She reached over to lay her fingertips gently on his knee. "I need you to go back and tell them that I made it here okay and that I'll be back in the spring. Will you do that for me?"

He looked down, conscious of her touch. "They'll throw me out for not trying to stop you."

She patted his knee, then withdrew her hand. "You know they wouldn't do that. And you *did* try to stop me. I'll tell them that when I get back. But do you really think you could have anyway? I could just wait until you fall asleep and be gone when you wake up."

She softened her voice. "Let's do this together, my way."

He looked at her, trying to understand her, then nodded slowly. "Okay."

He wanted to say something else but couldn't think of anything.

She lifted the lid off the pot and gave the contents a stir. "Just about ready."

They ate, then packed up their belongings, Ragan only taking what a refugee would have, then walked to the mouth of the cave. The day was grey with low clouds and the taste of snow in the air.

"What do you think these caves were for, anyway?" he asked, trying to make conversation to delay her departure.

She looked around at several other gaping entrances to the sides of them. "I don't know. They must have been excavated for storage or something and never used."

"I'm glad we found them."

She nodded, looking at the deserted highway in front of her then back at him. "Thanks for coming with me, Kyle. You've made the last few days better than they would have been."

He nodded, unable to speak around the knot is his throat.

She forced a smile. "You can buy me a beer when I get back, okay?"

"Okay," he nodded, his voice raspy.

"Bye," she said, turning and walking quickly toward the highway.

He watched her make her way across the divided highway, then over the berm on the opposite side. He waited for over an hour, hoping to catch another glimpse of her, but finally turned back into the cave to wait for darkness before he started back.

Descending the berm, Ragan worked her way through a swath of dense brush before coming out onto a broad blacktop parking lot littered with abandoned cars. A mammoth old factory of some kind, most of its windows broken out, loomed over the far end of the lot and smaller, similarly decrepit buildings sat in eerie silence beyond it.

She waited inside the brush line, surveying her new surroundings, then, seeing no movement, began to move around the large open space while staying within the brush and occasional stands of trees.

It felt warmer, and she wondered whether the temperature had risen or if she was just feeling the elevated energy of her own body. She consciously calmed herself and attempted to open all her senses as Christian had taught them to. Again, she tasted the coming snow and heard a scratching noise that she quickly saw was a squirrel scurrying up a tree. Seeing and hearing nothing else, she started off.

She moved quickly through the industrial area of abandoned buildings and salvage yards until she came to the fringe of hilled residential neighborhoods.

The houses were small and close together, most of them obviously no more than a couple of bedrooms behind a living room, and many showing signs of neglect and disrepair that preceded the collapse. Cars sat along the curbs of the narrow streets, in some cases almost blocking them, and occasional hills of trash, old toys and broken furniture dotted the small front yards. There was no sign of people and she moved on.

An hour of careful progress brought her to a wide boulevard on which sat a mammoth stone high school. Large areas of vacant space spread out in front of it and the playing field behind it caused it to dominate the area like a castle over its holdings. It was the kind of area she was looking for, and she entered the back door of a house looking out onto the boulevard to set up watch.

The interior of the house was dark and musty, and she made a quick check, finding nothing but old furniture, some basic housewares and a few clothes strewn about.

Whether the house had even been inhabited at the time of the collapse was impossible to tell.

She went to the front window and sat in a dusty chair looking out onto the street. The area would be good for what she had planned, at least it would be if Force had patrols here. She dug the last scout ration out of her pack and began to eat it as she thought about what might lay ahead.

She wanted to be discovered in an open area where she could be easily surrounded. If she had been seen in the neighborhoods, things could have gotten dicey because of the closer quarters, but the open area would make it easier for them to control and make it more understandable that she would give up without a fight or trying to run. She wanted her capture to be as controlled and peaceful as possible.

She chewed the ration bar slowly, thinking about Stonemont and the people there. She could see their faces, hear their voices, and remember the feeling of belonging.

She reveled in the thoughts for several minutes, then pushed them aside, emptying her mind and steeling herself for what was coming. Swallowing the last of the ration, she took a drink from her water bottle and stood up.

Opening the front door, she stepped out onto a small porch and down two steps to the walkway. It had started snowing again, but there was no wind and the flakes fluttered slowly of their own accord. She looked up and down the broad parkway and, seeing no one, started walking south.

She walked in the middle of the parkway, purposefully stumbling on occasion to make herself look weak and disoriented. She knew that it would be impossible for her to tell if she was being watched, so she concentrated on making sure that everything she did portrayed a lone refugee who had been struggling to survive.

She had considered the possibility that she might be seen by a rogue band that was not under Force's control, and for this she had brought only an old revolver for defense. It was one of many from Stonemont's armory that had been picked up from raiders, so it's absence wouldn't affect Stonemont's security readiness. Still, she knew from reports that this was unlikely, as Force was said to have firm control over the area between the Irish and the highway she had crossed.

The snow was building up and she was concerned that it would fill in her tracks, as they would be able to validate her story if needed.

She continued to walk down the center of the parkway, attempting to imitate the trudge of one who was on their last legs, and had made it about a mile before she heard the sound of an engine.

Squinting her eyes against the recently arising wind, she exaggerated the stumbling walk until she was sure those in the vehicle could see her dark outline against the whiteness and, suddenly changing her plan, collapsed face first into the snow.

She lay still as she listened to the sound of the engine slowing, then a second engine joining it. She felt the cold of the snow beneath her and knew that it would soon be sapping her own warmth to dangerous levels, but she willed herself to remain motionless.

She heard the engines idling for another minute before advancing toward her.

The sound of the tires crunching across the fresh snow drew closer to her and finally stopped a short distance away. Doors opened and a man spoke in an authoritative yet quiet voice, though his words were unintelligible to her.

The sound of footsteps approached then encircled her and the toe of a boot sunk into her side, not gently but not hard enough to cause injury, and she let out a faint moan that she hoped would sound semi-conscious.

Footsteps approached her head and stopped. She could sense someone squatting down and a hand grabbed her hair and pulled her head back. She fought to remain calm and still.

The man released her hair, letting her head fall back into the snow and stood back up. "Get her in the truck and let's get her back to Sarina."

Keeping her eyes closed, she heard footsteps around her, felt herself being rolled onto something and lifted from both ends, then carried a short distance before being loaded into the back seat of a vehicle. She concentrated on staying calm and limp.

The inside of the vehicle was warm, and she resisted the temptation to scoop out the snow that had found its way down her neck. She felt it starting to melt and run down her skin in cold rivulets as she tried to hear what the two men in the front seat were saying, but their voices were too low for her to distinguish their words.

They drove for what seemed to her to be about twenty minutes before stopping. She heard the engine shut off and the front doors open as the men got out, then both of the rear doors opened. One of the men shook her and she gave a slight moan. She had seen enough people returning to consciousness after one mishap or another to know how they acted.

"Still out," said one of the men. "Let's get her inside."

10

Andrew Carnes took one more look through the binoculars, then backed slowly away from the Ridge. When he was far enough back that he could get up to a crouch, he turned and headed down the hill.

It had been a week since they had left Stonemont, and, so far, the trip had been interesting to say the least. Their primary task was to scout the Ozarks, where it was felt a large number of survivors may live, but the number of contacts they had made along the way had been surprising. Small communities seemed to be everywhere.

They had made contact with small communities in Drexel, Archie, Creighton and Urich, then split from the South Carolina group at Clinton and followed Highway 13 south from there. An Amish community was thriving around Osceola, a church camp turned village around Collins and a Christian polygynist group around Bolivar. The last had been an unusual experience for them, seeing men with multiple wives, but all groups had been courteous, if careful, had willingly shared their thoughts and opinions, and wished the scouts well on their mission.

They had skirted Springfield, having been warned of its gang control by the Bolivar group, then continued south on Highway 65.

The former bedroom communities of Ozark and Sparta had shown little activity, and Branson, the once-bustling entertainment mecca looked like a ghost town with its main drag cluttered with abandoned vehicles in front of vacant restaurants and tourist attractions.

They had found little of interest in Branson, a town in which they had expected to find a certain level of activity, and headed south across the mammoth Table Rock dam to follow the shoreline of the lake.

The numerous marinas showed no evidence of being operational, understandable in the wintertime, but many of the occasional houses they passed showed signs of habitation with some people who were outside giving a wave and others just watching them pass. All in all, the area gave the impression of being peaceful and unworried about attack.

They had pulled off the highway onto a gravel road that led to an unmanned lookout tower and had their perimeter set well before dark. The view from the top of the tower was amazing, encompassing miles of the Ozark hills in every direction and the lake to the west, and Brandon had adjusted the watch cycle to allow every scout on the tower sometime through the night.

Supper had been completed and the off-watch scouts bedded down when the tower watch had reported the strange glow to the south. Brandon had ascended the tower to take a look, then dispatched a pod to determine the source. The pod included Andrew, who was now trying to figure out how to explain what he thought he had seen.

He made the last few yards down the hill to where the rest of the pod was spread out, waiting, then led them back to the tower.

He had refused to answer the questions about what he had seen, not wanting to endure the razz that he knew would come, until he was face-to-face with Brandon. And now, he was.

"Christmas lights," he said.

Brandon raised an eyebrow. "Christmas lights?"

Andrew nodded. "That's what it looked like. Christmas lights."

Brandon looked around at several other scouts who were sitting around the campfire, listening, then back at Andrew. "Christmas lights like you put on your house?"

Andrew shook his head. "Not like I'd put on *my* house. Like the guy did in that movie. I've never seen so many lights."

"On a house?"

Andrew shook his head again. "All over the place. It looks they're on a lot of buildings and along some roads too."

"Did you see any people?"

Andrew shook his head a third time. "No, but we were pretty far away."

Brandon looked into the darkness for a moment, drained the cup of coffee in his hand and stood up. "Let's go take a look."

With Andrew leading, they made their way back to the ridge from which he had originally seen the lights.

Crawling through the lower boughs of a pine tree until he could see over the ridge, Brandon brought his binoculars up to his eyes and whistled. "Well, would you look ... at ... that."

A number of large buildings and several smaller buildings twinkled with thousands of white lights. Across a narrow cove, dozens of cabins nestled on the hillside, their chimneys trickling smoke into the sky.

"I don't know whether it's pretty or weird," he said, lowering the binoculars.

"I'd say it's pretty weird," said Andrew. "Who puts lights on their buildings nowadays?"

Brandon brought the binoculars up to his eyes again. "Apparently, they do."

He swept the binoculars to the right where the lake reflected the setting moon, then back to the lights below him. A closer study revealed white single-story buildings along the closer shore of the cove with what looked like large log lodges overlooking them from the hill above. A classic white church with a steeple stood in middle of the area and a serpentine road ascended the hill through the trees above the lodges.

What appeared to be headlights caught his eye from across the cove and he watched as they moved along the side of the hill above the cabins. The lights disappeared, then reappeared as the vehicle came around to the near side of the cove and revealed itself to be a small shuttle bus.

He couldn't make out the logo on the side, but continued to watch it as it came across a wooden bridge, passed the church, and pulled into the parking lot, stopping in front of the largest white building. A man got out and walked inside.

"Anybody have any idea what this place is?" he asked the group without taking his eyes off the sight in front of him.

A couple of *nope*s and several silent shrugs indicated that none did.

He put the binoculars back to his eyes and visually tracked the road up the hill, then turned back to Andrew. "You up to a night of work?"

Andrew shrugged. "Sure."

"Good." He nodded toward the scene below him. "Circle around them and see where that road comes out, then scout it back to us. Think you can do that?"

Andrew nodded. "No problem."

"Good deal. We'll save you some breakfast."

Andrew awakened from not enough sleep and felt the boot nudge him again. Opening his eyes into slits, he blinked against the brightness of the sun and looked up to see Brandon standing over him.

Brandon moved in front of the sun. "Sorry, sleeping beauty. I let you sleep as long as I could, but I couldn't let it get too late. Did you find a way for us?"

Andrew lowered the hand he had raised against the sun, drew aside his blanket and stood up. He nodded.

"Yeah. We go back out to the highway and a few miles south, then through a big double gateway and down a long winding road." He stretched his back. "It's a cool looking place, like a resort or something."

"How long do you think it'll take us to get there?"

Andrew shook out the blanket and started rolling it. "I'd guess maybe fifteen minutes to get to the main gate."

"Was it guarded?"

Andrew finished rolling the blanket and snapped a bungee wrap around it. "I'd say more attended than guarded. There were people there, but they didn't look like they were there to keep out very big trouble."

Brandon nodded and looked up the road toward the highway. "Okay. Get yourself squared away and we'll leave in about twenty."

It took them closer to thirty minutes to break camp and get on the road, then another fifteen to get to the turnoff. A roundabout lay about fifty yards ahead of them, with a convenience store on their left and a large double-entry gateway looming on a rise to their right.

Brandon stopped before the roundabout, checking his mirrors to make sure the other vehicles had cleared the highway. Seeing a pickup and several people at the gas pumps of the convenience store, he looked over at Andrew. "Was anybody over there when you came through last night?"

Andrew shook his head. "Not that I noticed."

Brandon looked back at the convenience store. "It almost looks like they're getting gas."

Andrew nodded. "It sure does."

Brandon took his foot off the brake. "Let's go take a look."

They circled three-quarters of the way around the roundabout and slowly pulled into one of the drives of the convenience store. One of the men standing by the vehicle pulled the nozzle out of the truck's fill tube and replaced it in the pump.

Brandon smiled. "Well, I'll be darned."

"You want to fill up?" Andrew chuckled.

Brandon shook his head. "Let's have a look at things first."

He pulled around the lot so that the other vehicles could stay in formation behind him, parked along the edge of the lot and got out.

The pickup that had been at the pump was pulling away and a man wearing a red cap was wiping his hands on a blue shop towel and looking at him.

He walked toward the man, raising a hand in greeting. "Howdy."

"Howdy back," said the man. "Need some gas?"

Brandon stopped about ten feet from the man and shrugged. "Well, we're a ways from home and pretty much carry our own. We were just surprised to see a working gas station."

"That so?" said the man, stuffing the rag in his hip pocket. "Where you all from?"

"Over in Kansas, up around Kansas City."

The man's eyes hardened just a bit. "Kansas, huh? What are you doin' around here?"

Brandon caught the change in the man, the tone of the question being more interrogative than friendly, and he wondered whether it had more to do with them being from Kansas or being from around Kansas City. He'd keep that in mind for future contacts.

"We're scouts from a place called Stonemont. It's a community of freedom-loving people and we're out trying to find out if there's anybody else around like us." He nodded at the man's cap. "I like your cap."

The man looked at Brandon closely, obviously weighing his words, the nodded toward the lead truck. "And I like your flag. I know what it means."

Brandon nodded, again looking at the man's cap. "Do you think we can?"

The many looked wary. "Can what?"

"Make America great again?"

The man's eyes softened a bit and small smile curled his lip. "Well, son, our America around here is already great again. How about yours?"

Brandon shrugged. "We're tryin'."

"Tryin'? How so?"

Brandon looked off into the northwest, envisioning Stonemont. "We've stabilized things out in our counties and doing pretty well, but we have a bunch of the old politicians from Topeka and some of the cities trying to create a new state of Kansas and take us over. It's probably going to come to a fight."

The man's smile tightened. "Yep, sounds like politicians."

"How about around here?" Brandon asked.

The man's smile grew wiley. "Ozarkia runs pretty much the way it always did before those pin-stripers in Washington thought they could try to tell us how to live. Everybody does what they want to as long as they aren't hurtin' anybody else, minds their own business and helps their neighbor when it's needed. This so-called crash is the best thing that ever happened to us."

Brandon considered the man's words. "Ozarkia? Is that where we are?"

The man chuckled. "It's where you are, where you've been for a while, and probably where you'll be for a while longer. It's southern Missouri and northern Arkansas, give or take a here or there."

Brandon nodded, looking around. "Not meaning to get into your business, but what kind of government do you have?"

The man shrugged. "You won't get into my business any more than I let you, son. We pretty much have the government God gave us in the book. He was pretty clear about things, and if people just go by that you don't need much more."

"Do you have a government, though, with laws and police and things?"

The man shook his head, his smile growing friendlier with patience. "The Bible has the laws in it. Only lawyers can make it more complicated than that, and for no good reason, and the only lawyers we had around here are doing something else now."

He paused for a moment, recognizing the questioning look on Brandon's face,

"Let me ask you something. Do you think it would be right for you to rob my store?"

Brandon shook his head. "No, of course not."

"Why not?"

"Because it's wrong."

"Who says it's wrong?"

Brandon thought for a moment, a bit confused. "Well, it's just wrong to take somebody's property from them against their will."

The man chuckled. "I think I could keep you going on this for quite a while, but you see, people know what's right and what's wrong and you don't need a bunch of formalized, written-down gobbledygook to explain it. Normal people know it, and those who don't are taken care of one way or another."

He looked at Brandon. "How is it up your way?"

Brandon smiled. "Pretty much the same. We operate according to the Ten Commandments and the Golden Rule."

The man nodded, his smile widening. "Well, we're of a mind, then. Where are you headed from here?"

Brandon looked around. "We're supposed to go east through southern Missouri and northern Arkansas," he smiled, "Ozarkia, I guess."

The man smiled and nodded.

"Our boss figures there's probably a lot of like-minded people around here and he wants to get an idea of what's going on," Brandon continued. "He wants us to make contacts, too. For possible trade and such."

The man nodded. "Makes sense. What do you all have up there to trade?"

Brandon thought for a moment. He wasn't sure, exactly, what Jim had in mind as far as trading, but a few things occurred to him. "Well, we have wheat, cattle, buffalo and things like that."

The man nodded again. "Might be something there. Just might be."

Brandon looked toward the double-gated entrance across the roundabout. "What's that over there?"

"That's Big Cedar."

"Is that like a resort or something?"

The man nodded. "Used to be. Now it's a town."

Brandon gave a questioning look. "A resort turned into a town?"

The man nodded again. "Yep. Big Cedar used to be one of the top resorts in the country. First class all the way. When the crash happened, some of the people who were staying there just stayed. Over time, some of those who worked there moved into some of the lodges and cabins, and so did some other folks from around here. It got to be pretty much self-sustaining, and before you knew it people started thinking of it as a town if its own."

"You think it would be okay if we went in for a visit?" Brandon asked.

The man shrugged. "I don't see why not. Check with the guys at the gate and they'll give you a yes, a no or a maybe so."

Brandon looked back at the entrance, then back at the man. "Okay, thanks."

The man nodded. "Take care."

Brandon walked back to the truck and got in. "The guy says the place was a resort turned into a town."

"So, are we going in?" asked Andrew.

Brandon closed the door and put the truck in drive. "May as well."

11

They left the convenience store parking lot, again driving around the round-a-bout to exit onto the drive up to the large log gate. A large sign over the left entrance said Big Cedar Lodge. The sign over the right one said Top of the Rock. What looked like security checkpoints were in the stone supports on the right, left and center.

"Which one do we go through?" mulled Andrew.

Brandon saw a man wearing beige cargo pants, a brown jacket and a Bass Pro cap coming out of the left guard house. A handgun was in a holster on his right side. "I guess we'll go over there."

He drove toward the left entrance and stopped when the man held up his hand, then rolled down his window.

"Howdy," said the man, dropping his hand. "Welcome to Big Cedar. You all visiting?"

Brandon smiled at the seemingly innocuous greeting, though he was sure there were back-ups he couldn't see, and thought about how best to state their purpose.

"Well, yes and no. We're from a place up in Kansas making kind of a recon tour of what's around us. To be honest, we didn't know you were here until last night when we saw your lights. We just wanted to stop by and introduce ourselves and maybe see who you all were."

The man nodded thoughtfully. "Well, that's right neighborly of you." He looked at the vehicles behind Brandon's truck. "Kansas, huh? What part of Kansas?"

"Up around Miami County. South of Kansas City."

The man nodded again. "I've been up that way deer hunting." He chuckled. "Almost got nabbed by one of your game wardens for havin' more deer than tags."

He nodded at the flag mounted behind Brandon's cab. "That your flag?"

Brandon nodded. "Yeah."

The man tilted his head and looked at the limp flag more closely. "I can't quite make it out. What's it say?"

"Stonemont," replied Brandon. "It's on a Pine Tree flag."

"Oh," said the man, nodding. "Well, I'm familiar with the Pine Tree flag. What's Stonemont?"

Brandon recognized the soft interrogation. "It's the community we're from."

The man looked back at Brandon, then over at Andrew. "You all looking to move down here or something?"

Brandon shook his head. "No, we're fine where we are. Our boss just wants us to see who and what's around, make contacts and friends if we can and head back home."

The man nodded sagely. "Makin' friends is good business. You can never have too many friends."

He glanced at the other vehicles again, then back at Brandon. "I imagine our council wouldn't mind havin' a chat with you since you've come so far and can probably give us some news, but I don't think I can let all of you in right off. Would you be interested in just your vehicle goin' in for a first meeting, then we'll see how it shakes out?"

Brandon thought about that. It went against the grain to split the team, and the four of them would be on their own and out of contact with the rest. Still, he could understand the man's caution, and he was, after all, inviting them in. He nodded. "Sure, we can do that."

The man nodded. "Good. The rest of your people can park over to the side if they like while you're down at your meeting. The store across the way is open till six if they want anything. It only accepts what we call cedar chips in payment, but tell 'em to get whatever they like - Big Cedar will pick up the tab."

Brandon nodded. "Thanks, that's very nice of you."

The man shrugged. "It's nothing. We try to be nice until someone gives us a reason not to be. One more thing. I assume you're all armed?"

Brandon nodded again, afraid the man was going to ask them to leave their guns at the gate. "Yeah."

"I figured. Only a fool would go around unarmed, and you boys don't look like fools. We just ask that you leave any long guns in your vehicle and be polite with your handguns while you're in our town. Sound good?"

Brandon smiled, relieved. "Sounds good."

"Okay." The man stepped back and pointed to the gate. "Just pull on through there and I'll call for a guide to take you in."

They waited for only a few minutes until a white pickup with a Big Cedar logo on the doors came up the road, circled around and gave them a wave to follow.

"Well, that didn't take long," observed Andrew. "What kind of communications do you think they have?"

Brandon looked around and shrugged. "I don't know. Maybe we'll find out."

The road in was long, serpentine, and beautiful. Views from the switchbacks revealed the rugged surrounding hills and occasional glimpses of the sparkling lake ahead. Coming to the apex of the hill they were on, they passed under a wooden sign spanning the road that said *Welcome to Paradise*!

The lake spread out below them, a breathtaking panorama of open water and irregular coves disappearing into the distance, with marinas and lake houses dotting the shoreline.

Andrew sat up in his seat. "Wow. Have you ever been here before?"

Brandon shook his head. "We competed in Springdale and Fort Smith, but we never came up here."

"Yeah? What did you compete in?" asked Andrew.

"Rodeo."

Andrew looked at him, surprised. "Yeah? Like bull riding and stuff?"

Brandon smiled. "Yeah."

"You ever ride a bull?"

Brandon chuckled. "Not for very long."

They continued to follow the pickup as it descended the hill toward the lake, eventually making a sharp turn through another rustic gateway that announced entry into Big Cedar.

The road here was narrower, a single lane through tighter turns, and they slowed in order to keep distance behind the guide truck.

"Look at that!" said Andrew, pointing at a rustic metal sign hanging next to the road.

Brandon smiled at the sign that read *Ya' shoulda been here yesterday!* and the next one of three fish cut-outs that said *They were bitin like crazy*! "That's funny."

He looked around them. "This is a cool place."

They made another switchback then crossed a fast-running stream as they broke out of the trees into the open. A massive log-sided lodge loomed above them to their right and another on a hill in front of them.

"Wow!" said Andrew.

"You said that before," said Brandon. "Look at that."

To their left was a classical white church with a soaring steeple. White columns supported a sloping roof over the front porch and tall peaked windows ran the length of the church, each bracketed by black wooden shutters.

"Wow," repeated Andrew.

They crossed a second stream as they followed the bend of the road to the left, then drove through the intersection of another road before entering a parking lot in front of a low white building with a wide, windowed cupola rising from its center.

The guide truck parked against the split-rail fence of the mostly vacant lot and Brandon pulled in two spaces away. He looked in the rearview mirror at the two scouts in the back seat. "Just lay your rifles on the floor. We're in their world now, so we'll hope for the best but be ready for the worst."

The scouts nodded and they got out.

"That's quite an entrance," said Brandon to the guide who was walking toward them.

The man nodded. "I worked here for sixteen years before the crash and have lived here for the past year. I never get tired of the drive in. It always settles me down and reminds me of what's really important."

"What's that?" Brandon asked.

The man looked at him and smiled. "Knowing where you're going and not being in so much of a hurry that you don't enjoy the journey."

Brandon thought about that and nodded. "I see what you mean."

The man continued to look at Brandon for a moment and turned toward the building. "Let's get you in to meet one of the councilors."

Brandon smiled. "Sounds like I'm back in school."

They walked toward the main door, over which hung a sign that said Registration. Beneath that sign hung a smaller one that said Welcome Home.

The man led them through a double-doored entryway, holding the inner door open for them, and they found themselves in a large, richly appointed lobby.

A large registration desk ran the length of the room to their left, a smaller reception counter angled the corner to their right and huge beams supported the tall cupola from which a massive, multi-tiered iron and stained-glass chandelier hung. Leather chairs and couches dotted the lobby and warm light glowed from the numerous table and floor lamps around the room.

"Hi Burt!" said a smiling woman coming around the reception counter. "Are these our guests?"

Burt nodded. "All the way from somewhere in Kansas, they say."

The woman smiled at the scouts. "Well, welcome to Big Cedar! We hope you enjoy your stay!"

She turned back to Burt. "Roger's over by the fireplace. He said to go on over."

"Thanks Emma. You going to be at The Buzzard tonight?"

Emma gave a slight shrug and toss of her hair. "I might be. Are you?"

Burt smiled. "I might be."

"Well, then I might see you there."

Burt's smile got bigger. "Yes, you might."

He watched Emma walk away, then turned back to the scouts. "Follow me, guys."

They walked across the lobby, looking up at the towering chandelier as they passed under it, and approached a semi-circle of leather chairs in front of a corner fireplace. A middle-aged man wearing a dark green waxed coat, jeans and hunting boots rose from one of the chairs.

Burt led the scouts into the group of chairs. "Roger, these are the boys the gate called about. They say they're scouts from over in Kansas just drivin' through to see who's around and what they're doin'." He turned to the scouts. "Boys, this is Roger Elrod, one of councilmen."

Brandon stepped forward and extended his hand. "Brandon Woods, sir. Pleased to meet you."

Elrod accepted Brandon's hand with a nod. "You too, son."

Andrew offered his hand next. "Andrew Carnes, sir."

Elrod shook the hand with a nod. "Andrew."

The other two scouts offered their hands, each of which Elrod shook before waving to the chairs around them. "I think that's more *sirs* than King Arthur heard in that amount of time. Let's all sit down."

The scouts followed Elrod's lead as he sat down.

Elrod leaned back in the deep leather chair and stretched his legs out in front of him, crossing his ankles. "So, tell me what brings you boys to our fair town."

Brandon sat up straight, organizing his thoughts. Diplomacy wasn't really his thing, but he knew that this contact was important, and he needed to represent Stonemont well. He remembered something he had heard Naomi say, *don't try to fake it, just say it.*

"Well, sir, our boss, Jim Wyatt, sent us to do some reconnaissance through the Ozarks to see how everything was down here."

"Yeah? Why?"

The sudden and pointed question threw him back a bit, but he remembered Naomi's advice and pressed on.

"We've created a community of people at Stonemont who think the same way about things and we run according to the Ten Commandments and the Golden Rule."

"So, you're a religious community of some type?" Elrod asked.

Brandon shook his head. "No. Well, yes, in a way. But not like everybody has to believe the same thing."

"You said you're run by the Commandments and the Golden Rule. Does everybody have to abide by them?"

Brandon nodded. "Yes."

"Well, I'd call that believing in the same thing, wouldn't you?"

Brandon took a deep breath and wished that Naomi was there instead of him. He took another breath as he watched Elrod watching him and thought about what she would say.

"We use the Commandments as our laws and the Golden Rule as our expectation for how people should treat each other."

He was surprised and pleased with how smoothly that had come out and expected another question from Elrod that didn't come. Instead, Elrod just watched him.

"We've been able to contact other groups in the area and have formed a confederation of communities for mutual assistance and trade," he continued. "Earlier this year, two of our scout teams went to South Carolina and met quite a few groups along the way that are rebuilding. Jim figured there were probably a lot of communities down here that were rebuilding, and he wants to make contact with them."

Elrod leaned forward in his seat. "Why does he want to make contact?"

Brandon was beginning to feel more comfortable as he remembered some of the conversations at Stonemont before they left.

"Jim says that if the country is going to come back, it can't just be a bunch of isolated groups of people. There has to be contact between the groups, communication and commerce. He says that the good groups should work together to help each other and themselves."

Elrod nodded thoughtfully. "And you say you've been able to put together some communities up your way to do this?"

Brandon nodded. "Yes sir."

"And your people met other groups like this on their way to South Carolina?"

Brandon nodded again. "Yes sir. Quite a few."

Elrod rose from his chair, followed by the others. "Tell you what. Let's get you boys situated and we'll get together for dinner at The Buzzard."

He turned to Burt. "Go ahead and bring the others down and put them in some cabins."

He looked back at Brandon. "How many guys you got?"

"Twenty-four, sir."

Elrod looked back at Burt. "Put them in four of the lakeside cottages and get them fixed up for the night."

Burt nodded. "Will do."

Elrod turned back to Brandon. "Burt will get you taken care of. Just relax for the day and make yourselves at home. We'll send a couple of shuttles for you about sundown and bring you up for dinner."

He extended his hand. "Enjoy the day and let Burt know if you need anything."

Brandon took the hand. "Thank you, sir. We appreciate it."

Elrod nodded and held his hand out to Andrew. "I'll see you at dinner."

12

They made their way down the stairs with the sounds of *The Devil Went Down to Georgia* coming up from the bar.

Burt had taken them from the registration building to their cabins after waiting for the rest of the teams to be escorted down from the main gate and had gotten them squared away, telling them that he'd be back with shuttles at sundown.

The cabins were large, each accommodating six people with full kitchens and living rooms with stone fireplaces. Arranged along the shoreline, they were situated at the end on a long dead-end road, something Brandon suspected was by design. The lake stretched into the distance, the hills rose behind them, and they spent the afternoon relaxing and watching eagles drifting high above the lake, occasionally diving toward the water and rising from the surface with a thrashing fish in their talons.

Two shuttles had picked them up as the sun lowered beyond the opposite shore and they were now descending into The Buzzard Bar beneath the larger Devil's Pool Restaurant upstairs.

The bar was larger than they had anticipated, stretching into dark corners they couldn't immediately see, but the low ceiling gave its expanse an intimate feeling and they were aware of the noise they made as they filed in.

The singer, a man seated on a small stage with a guitar and wearing a cowboy hat, stopped playing as they entered and said, "Holy moly, it looks like we're being invaded! Hope they don't want to hear any Beyonce - I ain't that woke!"

Some in the crowd laughed as the singer broke into *Where the Stars and Stripes and the Eagle Fly*, and Burt led them back to some tables in the rear where Elrod was standing, waiting for them.

Elrod motioned for Brandon to sit next to him at a table already occupied by several other men and directed the scouts toward several large tables next to them. "Today is Saturday, boys, so you can have anything you want as long as it's steak."

He sat down and turned toward a waitress who was already putting glasses of water on the table. ""What are the fixin's tonight, Ellie?"

Ellie smiled. "Tonight, we have grilled Kansas City strip with smashed potatoes, charred brussels sprouts with bacon and bread pudding with whiskey sauce for dessert. The cooks do all the steaks medium, so if you like it medium-well, just eat the outside and give your middle to the ones who like it medium-rare - maybe they'll trade you."

She put the last glass on the table. "I'll bring out the fried pickles in a minute."

Elrod smiled. "Thanks, Ellie, and the council is pickin' up the tab for these boys tonight."

Ellie nodded over her shoulder. "Gotcha, Roger. I'll be back."

Roger turned to Brandon. "Did you guys get settled in okay?"

Brandon nodded. "We did. Those cabins are nice. Thanks again, we really appreciate it."

Roger waved it off. "You're welcome. We keep those cabins available for people passing through. You came at the right time."

He took a sip of his water. "The other guys are what you might call out of pocket right now. One's down in Harrison, one's having dinner at his folks' house and the other two are on an overnight with their kids."

103

He looked up and smiled at Ellie as she placed a platter of fried pickles on the table. "But they'll all be back in the morning for our weekly meeting, so if you'd care to come and let us pick your brain a bit we'll be happy to let you pick ours in return."

Brandon nodded. "Sure, that would be great." He looked around the bar. "I heard this used to be a resort or something, then became a town?"

Roger picked a fried pickle off the platter and took a bite. "Yep. Big Cedar used to be one of the top resorts in the country, probably the top one in the mid-west. First class all the way. It was developed by Johnny Morris, the guy who owned Bass Pro and Cabela's, if you know them."

Brandon looked surprised. "Yeah? I used to spend half my paychecks in those places."

Roger chuckled. "A lot of us did."

"So, does he own the town now?" asked Brandon.

Roger shook his head. "No. When everybody started congregating here after the crash he came down and said that he thought this place would be good as a town since resorts weren't really needed anymore. He had us put together a town charter and a town council, then gave title of the place to the town, including Top of the Rock, which we use as a lookout position and where we'll be having our meeting tomorrow."

Brandon thought about that. "He sounds like a great guy."

Roger nodded. "He is. He built an empire out of fishing and did a lot for a lot of people."

He took a sip of water to wash down the bite of pickle. "Have you guys made a lot of contacts so far?"

Brandon nodded. "There are a lot more people around than I thought there would be. Just about every town we've passed through has had some kind of organized community in it. Is it the same around here?"

Roger took another bite. "Pretty much. You'll find small communities all through Ozarkia. Everything from a few families to towns like ours." He shrugged. "Well, maybe not like ours, exactly, but towns of several hundred people rebuilding life."

"The man at the convenience store mentioned Ozarkia," said Brandon. "Is that the official name of this area?"

Roger chuckled. "Not that I know of. It's just one of those things that people started saying and it caught on."

"How big is Ozarkia?"

Roger shrugged. "That would depend on who you ask. Some will say it's only southern Missouri and Northern Arkansas. Other will say it also includes part of Oklahoma and a bit of Kansas. I can't see that it matters. I just figure it stops where the hills stop. Are you all trying to go all through it?"

Brandon picked up a fried pickle and looked at it, considering. "Jim just wants us to kind of make a loop through it and see what's going on. You know, are communities surviving, working together and rebuilding? Also, he wanted us to see if we could get a line on a Viking network down here."

Roger's eyebrows raised. "A Viking network?"

Brandon nodded, still staring at the fried pickle. "Yeah. Our teams that went to South Carolina ran into some in Georgia who helped them out. They said the originator of it lives somewhere in Arkansas."

Roger shook his head. "We're a little far south for Vikings, I think." He looked at Brandon looking at the pickle. "You ever had one of those before?"

Brandon shook his head. "Nope."

"You gonna try it?"

"I'm not sure. What's it taste like?"

"Like a fried pickle."

A large plate with a sizzling steak, a large mound of mashed potatoes and another mound of Brussels sprouts appeared on the table in front of him. "Here ya' go, hon," smiled Ellie, who then set a matching plate in front of Roger. "Anything else I can get you right now?"

Roger shook his head and she paused, looking at Brandon. "You tryin' to stare down that pickle?"

"He's tryin' to decide whether to try it," said Roger.

"Yeah? How long's it gonna take him?"

Roger shrugged.

Brandon looked up at Ellie. "What's it taste like?"

Ellie looked at him for a moment, then took the pickle out of his hand and popped it in her mouth. "Tastes like a fried pickle."

Roger chuckled as he picked up his knife and fork and began to cut a bite off his steak. "Ellie's a fast one. It takes some effort to stay up with her."

He nodded at Brandon's plate. "Better get busy. We've got a night ahead of us."

13

Jim leaned forward, placing the steel cup on the coals he had drawn out from the small fire to keep it warm, then looked out across the valley. Snow still clung to north-facing surfaces, but the recent warming combined with several days of sun had almost completely removed it from the southern and western slopes.

He could see cattle grazing all the way to the next line of hills, occasional larger dots signifying the bison mixed in with the herd, and imagined how it would look when the land-holds were established.

The log he sat on was placed on the spot where he and Kelly had decided to position the front door of their new home, overlooking the valley below and facing the sunset, and he conjured up a mental image of where each of the others' homes would be built.

He had begun coming up here shortly after bringing Kelly to the spot for the first time and enjoyed both the solitude of the ride and the coffee ritual that seemed to give him enough mental distance from daily demands to be able to focus on the more distant challenges he knew lay ahead. And he knew the challenges were many.

He picked the cup back up and took another sip, this time holding it between his gloved hands in order to feel its warmth. It occurred to him that being warm when the world was cold and dry when the world was wet were two of the best feelings in life and he thought about that for a moment, recognizing it to be a primal feeling of being protected from external threats. That made him think about his own childhood feelings of safety and comfort within the protective cocoon of his family, which made him think about his own kids.

The development of Stonemont, Jamestown and the satellite communities had provided safety and security to thousands of people since the collapse, and he was sometimes amazed at how it had all happened. It seemed to him as if he had not so much designed it as he had simply taken each obviously necessary step set in front of him, and it was not difficult for him to see God's hand in it all as he knew in his heart that he neither deserved the blessings he had received, nor on his own would have been able to develop the community of which he now found himself the leader.

He had hoped, even expected, that the coming of winter would provide a respite from threats coming from the new state, and it was on this expectation that he had sent the scout teams to South Carolina and down through the Ozarks. Now, a renewed terror campaign had been launched by the Army of New Kansas, the ferocity of which exceeded that of previous attacks, and Stonemont was left with fewer combat-ready scouts than he would have liked.

He took another sip, enjoying the feeling of the heat rising from the hot coffee, and thought about the horror of the most recent attacks.

As in the past, the raids were sudden, brutal and obviously designed to spread fear as reports of them spread. And, as before, most of the women and many of the children were missing when the destruction was discovered. What was different was the systematic terror campaign that seemed to be an integral part of the ANK's recent operations and the increasing size of their targets.

The slaughter of the townsmen had continued, but now bodies hung from highway overpasses reminiscent of the southern cartels. Signs bearing the words *Enemy of the State* were nailed to their chests and they were left to hang until the birds, weather and natural decomposition reduced them to almost unrecognizable masses of bones and sinew. An early attempt by two local farmers to cut down bodies of their former neighbors had been discovered and the farmers were hung from the bridge alive, the ropes fastened around their chests in order to avoid the quicker death of strangulation. ANK guards had remained posted at the bridge to ensure that no rescue could be attempted as the men took days to die of exposure and dehydration.

The targets were changing, too. Whereas before, the raids had concentrated on communities of a dozen or so families, more recent attacks had been against larger towns.

Whatever the ANK's intentions were, the results were clear. Larger communities no longer felt safe because of their size, and witnesses now survived to spread the message of terror. This last had provided a description of the man who was apparently the new field commander of the ANK, and it was the description of a man who reveled in the suffering of others.

Jim placed the cup back on the coals and stood up, stretching his back. He had been thinking about the situation with the ANK for some time, trying to decide the best course of action, but so far nothing had presented itself as a best course. The areas close to the other groups of the confederation were being affected, but Stonemont was still insulated from New Kansas by distance and the other groups, and it was the responsibility of the other groups to deal with situations in their areas anyway. Hopefully, the scout team he had sent to meet with the Fort Riley group would bring back some news.

He reached down and picked up the cup, bringing it to his mouth to take a sip, and saw what looked like smoke beyond the steam rising from the coffee. He lowered the cup and looked more closely, again seeing what appeared to be a thin trail of smoke at the base of the far hills.

Turning from the fire, he walked to where Ghost was tethered, removed a pair of binoculars from a saddle bag and turned back toward the valley, lifting the binoculars to his eyes.

It took him a moment to isolate the dust plume of the vehicles, the two pickups of the team that had gone to Riley, and he watched them for a moment before lowering the binoculars and tossing his coffee onto the ground. The team was two days early and coming fast.

Stashing the binoculars back in the saddle bag along with the cup, he threw dirt onto the fire, making sure that no embers were exposed, untied Ghost and mounted up.

It had been a long time since he had experienced the kind of foreboding he felt as he rode, and he pushed Ghost harder than usual as they made their way back to the compound.

They hadn't expected that the team would encounter any trouble on what was essentially a routine run to touch base with Wade Dorser out at Riley, but the earlier-than-expected return and the speed at which the vehicles were traveling couldn't mean anything good.

He guided Ghost up the hill overlooking Jamestown to make sure the team hadn't stopped there, but not seeing their trucks, pushed on to the compound. Ignoring the stable, he rode into the commons at a canter to see the pickups pulled up to the main hall, one of them backed in. A small group of people had gathered around the trucks and the scouts were standing in what seemed to be a protective ring between the crowd and the pickups.

He slowed Ghost to a walk as he approached the group, then stopped and swung off, dropping the reins and walking toward the scouts who stepped aside to let him through to the truck that was backed in. Rounding the rear of the truck, he looked into the bed to see a canvas tarp covering something beneath it.

Suspecting what he might find, he took a corner of the tarp in his hand and slowly drew the tarp aside to reveal what lay under it. He froze.

"They hadn't come back from their patrol," choked one of the scouts, his voice low and raspy. "We went looking for them and heard them screaming." He hung his head, his shoulders quivering. "By the time we got there it was too late."

Jim looked at the young scout, then at the others who stood in silence, their uniforms dirty and eyes hollow in faces drained of life. He looked back at the three charred bodies in the truck bed, pulled the tarp back over them and put his arm around the scout, who broke down into sobs.

He held the young scout for a moment, then, seeing Christian approaching, released the scout and walked to meet Christian before he reached the group.

Christian raised his chin toward the trucks. "What's up?"

Jim put his hand on Christian's shoulder and spoke quietly. "You'll see. Take them over to the scout barracks. Double up the home guard, get Mike and have him bring all of the scouts in, then ask Cassius and Doc Scheffler to meet us at the barracks.

Dave Scheffler entered the barracks office, his face drawn and eyes semi-glazed. He shook his head. "I've never seen anything like it."

He picked up a bottle of bourbon from the counter, poured an inch into a coffee cup and took a drink before turning to the group around the table. "You wanted to know what happened."

He shook his head and took another drink before continuing. "I can't be certain of the exact order of things, but they were partially skinned, their arms and legs were broken, and they were burned alive." He looked at Jim. "Do you need to know more than that?"

Jim looked at him for a moment. "You're sure they were alive when they were burned?"

Scheffler looked into his cup and nodded. "Yes."

Jim continued looking at the doctor for several moments, then turned to Mike. "I want all of the scouts to come in and view the bodies. The home guard too. I want every one of them to understand what we're dealing with."

Mike nodded.

Jim looked at Christian. "Kelly and I will go with Mike to tell their families. If you and Naomi would like to come with us, that would be fine."

Christian nodded. "Of course."

Jim turned to Street. "Cassius, I'd like you to come with us to talk to the families, then be here when the scouts and guards view the bodies. We'll go to the families in about an hour, then start bringing in the scouts and guards this afternoon."

Street nodded. "Okay."

Jim turned back to Mike. "Everything changes now. Keep an eye on the men as they view the bodies and let me know if you think any of them won't be able to function afterward."

He looked at Street. "I'd appreciate it if you would let me know too, Cassius. I don't want any of them going into critical situations if their head isn't right."

Both men nodded.

Jim paused for a moment, thinking about whether there was anything else that needed to be done right then, then looked around at the group. "Okay, let's go get Kelly and Naomi and go see the families. Then Mike can bring in the scouts. After they've come through, they can relieve the Home guard for them to come through."

He looked a Scheffler. "Dave, I'd appreciate it if you could stay with the bodies until Mike gets back."

14

The atmosphere was subdued as they gathered in the den, the lowered lights reflecting the moods of those assembled there and the heaviness of the room's furnishings providing the perfect background for the somberness of the moment.

The meetings with the families had been heart wrenching and had taken longer than they had anticipated because of the difficulty the families had, first in understanding and then accepting the news of their loved ones' deaths. Nothing had prepared them for this eventuality. Even though the scouts were understood to be the military of Stonemont, they had often seemed more like adventurers than soldiers, and the group had never suffered a loss such as this.

The pre-meditated brutality of the killings made it even more difficult for both the families and the scout corps as a whole to mentally process, and the entire community was in a state of shock and sober reflection.

By the time the scouts and home guard had completed their viewing of the bodies it was well after dark and a mood of sadness and anger covered the community.

Jim turned from where he had been staring out the window onto the commons and looked at Mike. "How many scouts do we have?"

Mike sat forward on the couch he was sharing with Christian and Naomi. "We've got a total of four hundred and sixty-two currently active, which is thirty-eight teams pulse six. Two of those teams are currently down in the Ozarks and one is in South Carolina. That leaves thirty-five and a half teams. The extra six can be folded in to replace the three we just lost," he paused for a moment, thinking about Ragan and the other scout who was missing and wondering how he should say it, then continued, "plus the two who are currently on special assignment."

"And how many in training?"

"Only about fifteen. We have a large group of over a hundred starting after the first of the year."

Jim nodded. "And how many qualified snipers?"

"Twenty-seven teams now have designated snipers, with the remainder having shooters who can shoot well enough for the designation but haven't completed all of the fieldwork yet."

Jim nodded slowly, thinking, then looked around at the group. "I had hoped that things could be put off until spring, but this has to be dealt with now. Waiting could just mean more innocent people being slaughtered."

He looked at Tom, his head of intelligence. "What's the current status of the ANK, Tom?"

"Their exact manpower is unknown," Tom answered, "though we estimate it at about three thousand."

"And it's current leadership?"

"Also unknown, although the elevation of recent raids suggests a change either in direction or operations. Since we don't have any I-Teams in the New State anymore, our information is sketchy."

"Do you want us to try to put another I-Team in?" asked Mike.

Jim shook his head. "No. We can't afford to wait the time it would take them to start generating information and I don't want to take the chance of any of our people being caught in the middle of what's coming."

He looked at Christian. "How strong are Freelove, McGregor and the Riley group?"

Christian thought for a moment. "Mark's group is strong but thin. I don't think he can spare many, if any, without leaving his own area open to attack. Same thing with McGregor. As far as Riley is concerned, I think they might be able to send a couple of dozen people at the most. They have more people than Mark, but they also have more area."

"How much do you think we can depend on them?"

Christian looked at his wife. "I think Naomi probably has a better feel for that than I do."

Naomi nodded. "Mark and McGregor are solid, as you know. Their limitations are in resources, not commitment. As to Dorser and Hersey farther west, they have a closer relationship to each other than they do to us, as you would expect. I think they would also come on board with a combined action, though I think their motivation would be relative to how close the action was to their areas."

Jim looked back at Tom. "How many fighters do you think they would bring?"

Tom shrugged. "Our info on them is a little shallower than I'd like. I'd guess anywhere between a hundred and two hundred between them. From what I've seen, their people are good folks, but their training and abilities aren't up to ours."

Jim nodded, thinking, then turned to Bill. "Bill, are you familiar with the concept of just war?"

Bill nodded. "We covered it in an international law class, and of course there have been many discussions about it concerning most of our, I mean the United States', military actions since Vietnam. I wouldn't claim to be in anyway an expert on it though."

"Bellum justum," said Tom. "First, it must be waged only as a last resort, after all peaceful means have failed. Second, it must be for a just cause, it must correct a grave, immediate, and ongoing evil. Third, it must come from a valid authority, arising from a consistent policy or principle. Fourth, it must have chance of probable success - so you can't send people into war when it would mean certain death. Fifth is proportionality - force must be proportionate to the situation and not more than necessary. And finally, there must be an exit strategy. There must be a defined goal and the war must be ended as quickly as possible."

Jim smiled. "I should have known our military people would know."

He looked around the group. "We have to act in order to stop the continued slaughter by the New State. Responding to individual attacks, whether as interceptors or hopeful rescuers is no solution to the problem the New State has made clear we face. And we cannot wait for it to arrive at our doorstep."

He paused, looking down into his coffee cup, then back up at the group. "We must destroy the forces that threaten us and those around us. I have no desire to simply contain them, as that would simply direct their attracts elsewhere and would allow them to be a continual threat to us in the future."

He looked at Bill and Cassius, who were seated on the same couch with Ann. "Bill, you are our legal counselor. Cassius, you are our spiritual counselor. I'd like your thoughts on the aspects of just war as Tom laid them out."

He looked around at the group. "I'd also like to hear anyone else's thoughts."

Everyone nodded and he turned to Tom. "Would you go through it again for us?"

Tom nodded. "The first is that it must be waged only as a last resort, after all peaceful attempts at resolution have failed."

The group sat quiet for a moment before Bill spoke.

"To be quite honest, I don't see how this applies. The New State, through its military arm, the ANK, have repeatedly attacked innocent people, killing in the most heinous ways and presumably taking captives for who knows what reasons. I think this puts us far beyond attempts at peaceful resolutions. What are we supposed to do, ask them to stop? Offer them some kind of payment if they stop? I hardly think so."

Jim looked at Tom, who nodded in agreement, then looked around at the group." Anyone else?"

Everyone shook their heads.

"Okay, Tom, what's the second one?"

"It must be for a just cause, correcting a grave, immediate and ongoing evil."

Jim looked around the group again. "Is there anyone who would argue against action on those grounds?"

Again, the group shook their heads.

"What's next, Tom?"

"That it must come from a valid authority, arising from a consistent policy or principle."

Cassius spoke up. "Who so sheddeth man's blood, by man shall his blood be shed; for in the image of God made he man."

Everyone looked at Cassius.

"Genesis 9:6," Cassius said. "God's directive to Noah. I believe there can be found no more valid authority, nor a more consistent policy or principle than God's own word."

Everyone was quiet, absorbing the words and their meaning.

Finally, Jim turned back to Tom. "I happen to remember the fourth. It must have a chance of success." He looked back and forth between Tom and Mike. "I think we can succeed with the right plan. What do the two of you think?"

Tom and Mike looked at each other, then both nodded.

Jim nodded. "Good. Then I'm going the address the final two, which I also happen to remember. First, proportionality. There will be no proportionality. We will destroy the New State and the ANK completely, and we will do it in such a way that will pose as little risk to our own people as possible and in a manner that no one who hears about it will want to try this again."

He looked closely at his head of intelligence and head of scouts, then around at the others. Nods and several grim smiles assured him that everyone supported what he had just said.

"I would say that *is* proportional," said Bill. "They have slaughtered whole communities. I would call their complete destruction preoportional."

"I would agree," said Tom.

Jim nodded. "Good. And finally, our exit strategy is simple. We will not be exiting. We will cease offensive action only when all ANK and New State officials have been eliminated."

The silence in the room continued, accompanied by nods of agreement and he waited a minute before continuing.

"This is a departure from the way we have done things in the past. Before, we have acted either in defense or preemptively in order to forestall or interrupt specific expected attacks. This is the first time we will be initiating offensive action on a major scale against an enemy that has not attacked us directly. However, I'm not willing to sit by and wait for them to come for us while watching them continue to pick off small communities in preparation. Does anyone have any questions, comments or concerns?"

The group continued to be silent until Bill asked, "Do you intend for the state of New Kansas to be done away with, then?"

Jim nodded his head. "Yes. There's no reason to try to fix it. It was started by the wrong people for the wrong reasons and serves no good purpose. I'm going to propose that the state we will establish be known as The Republic of Kansas."

Bill looked at him closely. "A republic?"

Jim nodded. "Yes."

"There are republics and there a *republics*," Bill said thoughtfully.

Again, Jim nodded. "I've been doing some studying on that, from Polybius to the transition from an aristocratic republic to a democratic republic in the United States in the early eighteen-hundreds."

Bill's eyebrows lifted. "You *have* been doing some studying."

"And I've learned a lot that I wasn't aware of, or at least knowledgeable about. And I doubt most people are."

"And what have you decided?" asked Bill still watching him carefully.

Jim looked around at the group. He hadn't intended to reveal the details of his plan just yet, but maybe this was the time to share the basic framework. He took a sip of his coffee before beginning.

"The word republic comes from the Latin words *res* and *publica*, meaning, essentially, a matter of public concern. As it relates to governance, it signifies that a government derives its authority from the people and their representatives as opposed to a monarch."

He set his cup on the sideboard before turning back to the group.

"The United States was founded as what was originally considered to be an aristocratic republic. That meant that the leaders and representatives came from that part of society it was felt was best able to govern because of their education and experience and elected by those who represented the producing class - essentially landowners. The result was the creation of what became the greatest country ever known."

He paused for a moment, allowing that information to sink in.

"That began to change in the 1820s when a mood of egalitarianism started to bubble up in the country. The idea that everyone should have an equal vote, regardless of their knowledge of civic affairs or their contribution to the community or society in which they lived started to supplant the more restrictive aristocratic model."

He looked at Bill. "What would you say has been the result?"

Bill shrugged. "That's a complicated question."

Jim nodded. "I guess it is. Let me put it more simply. Notwithstanding technology, which period would you say was superior as far as common knowledge, common sense, common morals, common manners and culture, family unity, religious observance, individual responsibility and desire for self-determination, the late seventeen-hundreds or late nineteen-hundreds?"

Bill thought for a moment. "I'd have to say the seventeen-hundreds."

"And why is that?"

"Well, as indicated in the question itself, the people held greater commonality in knowledge, values and ethics."

"And they had a more intelligent and informed voting population," interjected Kelly.

Jim picked his cup back up. "Exactly right. You can see the rise and fall of The United States in the changing demographics of its voters." He took a sip. "And if you study history, you find that universal suffrage invariably brings about the collapse of a nation."

"You don't want there to be universal suffrage in the new republic, then?" asked Ann.

Jim shook his head. "No. Voting rights should be determined according to contribution."

"I agree," said Kelly. "There should not be equal say or representation if there isn't equal contribution. That's what caused so many of the problems before."

She paused, thinking. "However, we can't allow those who control all of the land to become tyrants over those who have less."

Jim nodded. "I agree. So, what's the answer?"

He looked around the group, understanding that they all had questions, but knowing that this was not the time to go into it further.

"We'll talk about the details later," he said. "Right now, the important thing is to remove the immediate threat and establish the foundation on which we can hopefully build a republic that will truly represent and serve the needs of it's citizens."

He set his cup back down. "We'll have services for the deceased scouts tomorrow. If the rest of you could attend to the details, I'd like to talk with Christian, Naomi, Mike and Tom for a bit about operations."

The group nodded and stood up quietly, each conscious of the changes being forced upon them.

Jim watched as the others filed out, then walked to the couches and sat on the opposite end of the one on which Christian sat. He looked around at the others.

"We will, of course, notify the other groups of our intentions and welcome any participation on their part, but I don't anticipate that will be much."

"The extent of their contribution will tell us a lot," said Tom.

Jim nodded. "Yes, it will. I know that Mark and McGregor won't be able to provide much, but if they can help with a security line around here it will help."

"I imagine Wade Dorser will bring some from Riley, and Hersey should bring some from farther west," offered Christian, "though who knows how many that might be."

"They should," said Jim, "but should and will aren't always the same thing. I think Wade is solid, but Hersey might feel it's a bit too far from his border for him to get involved."

"I doubt that he understands the importance of it," said Tom. "I know that he gets most of his information from Wade, and I know that Wade doesn't run much active Intel gathering. A percentage of a percentage may not be very convincing."

Jim looked at Naomi. "What are your thoughts?"

Naomi thought for a moment. "Wade and Hersey have always been strong in their assurances of mutual assistance. Of course, that was when the need was an abstract. Reality will put that to the test." She paused. "Would you like me to go out and meet with them?"

Jim glanced at her expanding belly and shook his head. "No, this is no time for you to be going out on things like this."

"I can go," said Tom. "I can leave in the morning with a scout team, swing wide of the threat area and be at Riley by tomorrow afternoon. It might take a couple of days to get an answer from Hersey, but I should be able to get an idea of what we can expect from them."

Jim nodded. "That would be good."

He looked at Mike. "Pick a team to go with Tom. Then, we need to find out where the ANK is. I don't want any small groups going out now. Make each group at least a hundred people and send them out to track down the ANK. When we find them, we'll bring the groups together and decide how best to proceed."

Mike nodded. "Eight teams will make ninety-six scouts in a group. We can send out four groups and have some spares. Is that okay?"

Jim nodded and stood up. "That's fine. Let's get moving on it. There are people out there depending on us, whether they know it or not."

15

Patrik Torkelson held his hands out to the fire in front of him and tried not to think about the one behind him.

The temperature had dropped to the point where he had finally put on a sweatshirt, an old grey one he had worn when he had billed himself as "The Best Darn Carpet Cleaner in the Twin Cities." Most of the screen-printed logo had worn off long ago, though the large "C" of "Classic" could still be faintly seen, and it reminded him of his previous life, a time of both happiness and frustration before the collapse had brought out his hidden qualities and abilities.

He heard some of the men talking, their voices muffled by both bitterness and the wind, and thought about the day.

They had come on it by accident, having taken what they thought would be a shortcut to where they had heard one of Samatar's raiding parties had been spotted. At first, they had thought it to be some kind of religious display, an intricate though horrendous life-size copy of Nero's Torches, a depiction of the Roman Emperor's burning of Christians to light his garden, but as they drew closer, the true horror had revealed itself.

It had taken them the better part of the day to remove the burned corpses from the stakes to which they had been tied and move them to a communal pyre for burning since the ground was too frozen to dig graves. The lucky ones had been fully engulfed by the flames, their final screams frozen in the open mouths and tortured twists of a human body straining for release from a pain beyond endurance. The less fortunate had been only partially burned, apparently from lack of enough fuel stacked at their feet, and had been left to die from shock and exposure after their fires had gone out. How long their suffering had lasted was impossible to know and he tried to push it from his mind even as their communal pyre warmed his back.

A dark form appeared from beyond the firelight. "It looks like they're headed toward Iowa, Tork."

Patrik continued watching the flames in front of him for a moment before looking up. "Why would they go to Iowa? It's full of pigs."

Aksel shrugged. "I don't know."

Patrick looked back into the fire. "They're going south for warmer weather and more slaves."

Aksel stood motionless, saying nothing.

Patrick rose to his feet and looked back at the pile of burning remains. "Have the men get some sleep. We'll head south in the morning."

16

Brandon cinched the strap tight on his bedroll, picked up his pack and walked outside to where the rest of the scouts were loading the vehicles.

They had stayed longer than he had intended, but the hospitality at Big Cedar and growing friendships with the locals had extended their stay to a little over a week and he was glad that it had.

The area had come back from the collapse in remarkable ways. Blessed with the resilient Ozark spirit, the people had come together to preserve, then rebuild, a web of communities throughout Ozarkia that provided a peaceful and productive environment for its residents. Without central government control or intervention, the people had fallen naturally into life patterns that promoted what was good and purged what was bad - the latter often accomplished through individual actions and sometimes communal.

The mystery of the lights had been solved when they learned that engineers and workers from the area had been able to retrofit one of the turbines of the Table Rock Dam with pre-electronic parts and the delivery of electricity was growing slowly throughout the area as parts on the distribution lines were replaced.

During the days they had fished, visited with and gotten to know more of the residents, met with the town leaders on matters of security and trade, and traveled with them to other small communities in the area. At night they had relaxed and eaten at The Buzzard.

"Sure you want to leave, boss?" Andrew joked as he approached the lead vehicle. "Things are gettin' kind of comfortable around here."

Brandon smirked. "Yeah, and I've seen who you've been getting comfortable with."

He put his pack in the truck bed. "You know that long distance relationships never work, don't you?"

Andrew shrugged. "Maybe, but I figure the fun is in the tryin' - at least for a while."

Brandon chuckled. "I guess so."

He looked down the row of vehicles. "Everybody ready?"

Andrew nodded. "Yep. Rarin' to see what's around the next bend."

He looked up the road. "Here comes Roger to see us off."

Brandon watched as Roger's white pickup approached and stopped on the other side of the road. Roger got out, along with another man, and walked toward him.

Brandon raised his hand. "Morning Roger. You giving us an escort out?"

Roger smiled. "Mornin', Brandon. You're picken' a bad day to leave. Burnt ends and cornbread at The Buzzard tonight."

Brandon chuckled as the two men stopped a few feet away. "That's tempting, but I'm sure it'll be something just as good tomorrow and then we'd never get out of here."

Roger shrugged. "Well, you hit us on the way back then."

Brandon nodded. "You can count on it."

Roger nodded toward the man next to him. "Jeremiah wanted to come down to have a word with you before you left."

Brandon looked at the man. He had seen him around a number of times but had never been introduced or talked to him. He nodded.

"Word has it that you're wantin' to meet PJ," said Jeremiah.

Brandon looked from the man to Roger and back again. "Who?"

"PJ," repeated Jeremiah. "Pastor Joe."

Again, Brandon looked from Jeremiah to Roger and back again. He shook his head. "I guess I'm not following."

Jeremiah looked mildly irritated. "Pastor Joe. The head of the Viking network?"

A look of understanding flashed across Brandon's face. "Oh, yeah. You know anything about him?"

Jeremiah nodded. "I'm going to see him right now."

Brandon looked surprised. "He lives around here?"

Jeremiah shook his head. "Nah. He's down in Arkansas. But it's on the way you're goin' anyway."

"And you'll take us to him?" asked Brandon.

"I'll take you *toward* him. Then I'll tell him what I know about you and if he wants me to, then I'll take you to meet him."

Brandon looked at the man closely. "What do you know about us."

Jeremiah smiled. "Been watchin' you ever since you got here, and Roger and the rest of them have passed their verdicts on to me. So, do you want to or not?"

Brandon looked around at the scouts readying their vehicles, then back at Jeremiah and nodded. "Yeah, I want to."

Jeremiah nodded. "Well, we best be gettin' goin' then. I'll be takin' you in kind of a circly way with some stops here and there. We ought to be there in a few days."

"I thought you said you were going to see him right now," said Brandon.

Jeremiah half-closed his right eye. "I am *goin'* right now. But I'll see him when I see him. Still want to come?"

Brandon looked at Jeremiah closely, then nodded. "Let's go."

17

Kelly lay in the dark and listened closely for the sound of Jim's breathing. Not hearing anything, she slowly reached out and placed her hand gently on his back. At first, she felt nothing, then, finally, felt his back expand in a slow deep breath.

A smile came to her lips and she thought about how she had often done that very thing shortly after they had gotten married. He had slept so quietly then that she had to touch him to reassure herself that he was breathing. A silly thought, but marriage had brought about many interesting changes for both of them.

Leaving her hand on his back, she lay on her side facing him and thought about the years now behind them; the apartment where they had first lived, their year-long search for the perfect house, the birth of each of the kids and the long search for the property that became Stonemont. She remembered the first time they had driven up here, the kids running through the woods screaming, and the picking up of the thousands of rocks that became much of the house and had given it its name.

The move had been their dream, living in the close-in country on their own hilltop where Jim could write books and she could build her custom soap business while giving the kids the chance to learn and enjoy the skills and pastimes of the outdoors. And for a while it had been just that. Then, the collapse had happened.

Even after the collapse life had been good. They had been well prepared, and when Christian had shown up with the Garners it had seemed almost normal. Even as things progressed and the communities expanded it seemed like things were just going along as they should, directed by an unseen hand - and whose hand it was they had no doubt. But now there was trouble on the horizon beyond anything they had dealt with before, and it was something she knew could threaten their very existence.

She turned over carefully so as not to wake him, gently pulled the sheet and blankets off herself and slipped out of bed.

The faintest grey on the eastern horizon told her that the sun would soon be coming up and she quietly made her way to the door which she opened slowly before stepping through and closing it softly behind her.

She crept down the stairs and walked to the kitchen in her bare feet before turning on lights above the stove, sink and island, then opened the fire box of the stove. Seeing embers still glowing from the previous night's bank, she softly blew them into a flame, then added a handful of kindling and larger split wood before closing the door.

Crossing to the outside door, she opened it and stepped onto the cold stone of the veranda, removed a metal jug of fresh milk from the cold box and hurried back inside. Taking a medium size saucepan from the hanging rack, she filled it halfway with milk and set it on one of the cooking grates to warm up.

"You're up early."

She started at the sound of his voice and turned to see him standing in the doorway. She smiled. "I was just making myself some hot chocolate. Would you like some?"

He walked into the kitchen shaking his head. "Maybe after my second cup of coffee."

He walked over to her, put his arm around her and kissed her on the forehead. "What got you up so early?"

She shrugged. "I don't know. I just woke up and started thinking about things."

"Yeah? What things?"

She snuggled under his arm. "Just things."

He waited for her to say more, but when she didn't, he asked, "About the new state?"

She nodded against his chest, then looked up at him. "How bad do you think it's going to be?"

He thought for a moment, stroking her hair. He didn't want to tell her his true thoughts but knew that keeping them from her would serve no purpose. And she needed to know. "I think it's going to be bad."

"Do you think it's going to come here?"

Again, he took a moment before answering. "That's impossible to say. I hope not. We're going to do everything we can to keep that from happening."

She backed out of his embrace. "I have an idea that I don't know if you'll go for."

"You want to paint the front door blue again?"

She gave him a mock glare. "Seriously. I think all of the men and women not actively in the scouts or home guard should be taught how to shoot and train a bit on community defense."

He looked at her with interest. "And what gave you that idea?"

She shrugged. "Things are getting more dangerous. Our scouts are going to have to leave to fight the ANK, leaving Jamestown and Stonemont protected only by a skeleton force. We have several thousand people around here who may not be on the level of the scouts, but they should be able to put up some kind of defense if necessary, if they have weapons and a little training."

She paused. "I know how you feel about compulsory service, but all of these people benefit from the safety of the community. Shouldn't they all be expected to help defend it if necessary?"

He continued looking at her as he thought. It was true that he had always been against compulsory public service, feeling that it implied a degree of communal ownership of the individual, but he realized that bringing the residents into some kind of organized defense force could be useful - and might even be necessary.

"Have you thought about how it should be done?"

She nodded. "I think we should call a meeting of all of the residents and explain the situation to them, including the full extent of the threat from the new state and the need for community defense. The response will show us who's willing to step up and who isn't. Then we start training those who are willing and decide what to do with those who aren't."

He looked at her closely. "And what exactly do you mean, *do with them*?"

She turned toward the stove to check the pan of warming milk to give herself time to form her words, then turned back to him.

"Everyone who lives in our area benefits from the communities we have built or helped to build. If they had remained on their own, they would either be dead or struggling to survive. They came here for the safety and benefits our communities provide, and they should be willing to contribute to their defense."

She paused, looking him squarely in the eye. "If they don't want to help protect the community they benefit from, there are plenty of places outside our area where they can go and try to do it on their own."

He nodded slowly. "You've been thinking about this for a while, haven't you?"

She turned back to the stove and took the pan off the cooking grate, setting it to the side. "Yes, and there's something else. I've been hearing some things in town that I don't like."

His brow furrowed. "Like what?"

She turned back to him. "Do you remember that college professor who tried to start that trouble a while back?"

He nodded. "Yeah. I forget her name, but I remember her. I thought she had left."

She shook her head. "Nope. She works part-time at the pizza restaurant. The owners let her have weekly meetings of a group she has built up after the restaurant closes."

"Yeah? What kind of group?"

She turned back to spoon cocoa and sugar into the pan of milk. "It's called Citizens for Equity," she said, starting to whisk the contents of the pan. "Their motto is Equality for All. I'm sure you can guess what their agenda is."

He walked to the stove, moving the large enamel coffee pot onto the grate from which Kelly had removed the pan. "How long has this been going on?"

"Several months, apparently. I just found out about it for sure yesterday. I meant to tell you, but then we got to playing Monopoly and I forgot about it."

"How many people are they having at their meetings?"

She stopped whisking the hot chocolate and filled a mug from the pan. "I'm not sure. The person who told me about it said it was a good-sized group. Enough to almost fill the restaurant."

He opened a cabinet and took his pine tree mug off a shelf. "Did they tell you anything else?"

She shook her head. "Not much. She said she had heard about it from a neighbor who goes to the meetings, but she's never been herself."

She took a sip of the hot chocolate. "She said she wanted to tell me because she thinks the group is going to try to cause trouble for us and she and her husband don't like that."

He opened a canister and spooned a measure of Folgers instant into the mug. "Good. I'm glad she let us know."

"You want me to ask her to start going to the meetings and let us know what's going on?"

He nodded. "Yeah. And see if you can find someone else you trust to go too, but don't tell them about each other. I'll let Tom know and ask him to send someone in too."

"Don't you think she might get suspicious at her suddenly growing membership?"

He shook his head. "Not if they go in at different times. These kinds of groups believe so much in their idiocy that it's easy for them to believe others do too. Back before the change, the membership numbers of extremist groups were vastly inflated due to all the federal undercovers and informants joining. Just make sure that the two don't know each other or suspect that there is another informant there. That lets us double check the information and the informants."

She nodded. "Okay. How about my other idea?"

He leaned against the counter, Crossing his arms across his chest. "Would you like to be the one who announces it to the people."

She shook her head emphatically. "No, you're better at that stuff than I am."

"But it's your idea."

"Yeah, but I'm an idea person. You're a doer person."

He chuckled. "A *doer* person?"

She smiled. "Yeah. You're a doer."

"So, you don't believe in your idea?"

She shot him another mock glare. "Of course I believe in it. Otherwise, I wouldn't have suggested it."

He shrugged. "Well, it seems like you'd do it if you really believed in it."

She watched him as he turned around and poured simmering water from the pot into his mug. "Okay, I'll do it."

He turned back around, smiling. "Do what?"

Her eyes narrowed in semi-pretend irritation. "I'll explain it to the community."

He took a sip from his mug and smiled. "What a great idea!"

She gave a mock scoff. "Yeah. Glad I thought of it."

He laughed. "Me too."

"Okay, I'll talk to both her and Jenny today. Would you like an omelet?"

He nodded. "You bet. I'm going to take a quick shower and I'll be ready in twenty."

She watched him leave the kitchen with his cup of coffee and turned to remove six eggs and a thick bacon slab from the cool box.

The hens were laying almost as well as they did during the summer due to the lights that had been installed in the chicken house, and the kids now had a thriving egg delivery business in Jamestown. Coupled with the agreement they already had with the bakery and the Jamestown Inn, it had almost outpaced what they could supply, and Aedan was now talking about building another chicken house to increase production in the spring.

She shook her head at the thought. Only a few years before, the kids had been busy with school, theater, hockey and soccer. Now, they were running and building a business of their own.

She cracked the eggs into a stoneware bowl, tossed the shells into the compost bucket and added milk to the eggs. Setting a large cast iron skillet on a second cooking grate, she cut several thick strips from the slab, laid them in the skillet, then returned the slab to the cool box.

Her thoughts drifted to their conversation as she went about preparing the omelet mixture, which led to her thinking about the threats they now faced.

Life after the change had been challenging, exciting and sometimes even exhilarating. The tasks associated with developing and maintaining the communities had been far beyond anything she would have before imagined, let alone anything they would have experienced in a non-changed world. Still, it had for the most part been local in nature. The threat from the new state and the ANK was different and could destroy everything they had worked for.

She picked up her cup of cocoa and took a sip as she watched the bacon begin to sizzle, wondering what the reaction of the community would be to her suggestion.

She thought that most would understand the need and be happy to step up, but she figured that some would probably object. Although they had been in danger of starvation when they came to Stonemont, that memory had no doubt faded in the minds of many as life got easier and more secure. The question would be what to do with those who resisted participating in community defense. That was something that needed to be decided before making the announcement.

A soft glow coming through the windows made her turn to see the first tinge of sunrise and she thought about how difficult it often was to distinguish between a sunrise and sunset if you didn't know what direction you were facing. She wondered what direction they were now facing as a community, and whether it was the rising or setting of Stonemont.

18

Craig Peterson looked up from the broken board he was repairing on the chicken house to see what had caught his eye. At first there was nothing, then a momentary flash far up the road from his property. He straightened up, shielding his eyes against the afternoon sun, and watched.

He remembered the days when he could make out details at a distance, but those days were long gone and now he had to get closer to something or let it get closer to him, so he waited.

It took several more flashes before he recognized them as reflections from the sun and could make out the line of vehicles in the distance and he dropped the board and headed toward the house.

"Hi daddy!" yelled his young son as he came around the corner of his work shed.

He smiled. "Hey buddy, whatcha doin'?"

His son tossed a pebble into the air and swung at it with a piece of scrap lumber, missing. "I'm trying to hit rocks into the pond."

Craig stopped and looked toward the pond. "Havin' any luck?"

The boy shook his head. "Not much. I think I need a bigger board."

Craig smiled. "Yeah, maybe. Hey, do you remember the code orange drill we do?"

The boy let the pebble he had just thrown into the air drop to the ground without swinging at it. His eyes widened. "You mean strangers coming?"

Craig nodded. "That's right. We have a code orange. Do you remember what to do?"

The boy nodded seriously. "Yessir!"

Craig nodded toward the house. "Okay, go ahead."

The boy nodded again, emphatically. "Yessir!"

Craig watched the boy run toward the house yelling, "Code orange! Code orange! Mommy, code orange!", then turned toward his pickup to get his rifle.

Vehicular traffic wasn't entirely unheard of anymore, now that more vehicles had been retrofitted or rebuilt, but multiple vehicles this late in the day were rare and he was a careful man.

Retrieving his rifle from the truck, he walked down his drive into the woods, then up a berm that overlooked the last horseshoe turn of the road before it ran past his driveway. Reaching the top, he settled down behind a firing position he had constructed out of sandbags and concrete blocks.

He brought his rifle up and looked through the scope, waiting for the vehicles to clear a line of trees and come back into view. Flashes through the branches revealed what looked like a white flag on the lead vehicle, but he couldn't make out the pattern.

He shifted his scope to the spot where the lead vehicle would be emerging from the trees and thought about what would be happening in the house. Their code orange dictated that his wife and father-in-law take up firing positions in the house from which they could support him while his mother-in-law took the boy out the back door to a small bunker they had constructed in the woods. If there was trouble, he, his wife, and his father-in-law would try to protect the property from their initial positions. If he was overrun, his wife and father-in-law would fall back to the bunker in the woods and determine the best action from there. It wasn't a perfect plan, but it was the best they could do with what they had.

The lead vehicle emerged from the tree line and he counted as others followed. One after another they became visible until he counted over twenty and stopped counting. Over that number didn't matter, as there were simply too many to fight. His only hope was that they passed by. His palms began to sweat and he started praying.

The column drew closer and he still couldn't make out the flag on the lead vehicle, which he now saw was a red pickup that was slowing down. His heart sank as he saw the column reduce speed to a crawl, then stop at the gate to his drive.

He thought about falling back to the house and leading his wife and father-in-law to the bunker but kept his scope on the lead vehicle stopped at his gate.

The driver's door of the pickup opened and a man stepped out looking up at the hill toward his position.

The man gave a large wave meant to be seen from a distance. "Craig!", the man yelled. "Craig Peterson!"

Craig remained silent and flicked off the safety. Whoever they were, they knew his name, but he didn't recognize any of the vehicles. If they started to come toward him, he would have to make a decision. He didn't want to shoot anyone he didn't know, but there were too many of them to fight off and he couldn't allow them to get too close to his family before engaging.

"Craig Peterson!" the man yelled again.

Craig placed his finger on the trigger, put the first pound of pressure on it and centered the scope's reticle high on the man's chest. He took a deep breath, let half of it out and held the rest, waiting.

"Craig Peterson!" the man yelled again. "It's Stonemont and Le Chenes! What's for dinner?"

19

Craig walked back into the circle of firefight and sat in the folding chair between Aaron and Augustus. "The little guy didn't want to go to bed. He was too excited about you all being here."

Augustus smiled. "He's a cute kid. I remember when mine were that age. Wish we could go back and do it all again."

Craig accepted the cup of coffee Aaron handed him and looked around at the scouts and Le Chenes troops readying their ring of vehicles for the night. "I wish we could offer you better accommodations. We do okay, but just for ourselves. We're not exactly set up for company."

Augustus waived the thought away. "We're well situated, Craig. This set-up is becoming like home to us and Stonemont supplied us well for the trip."

"Sorry we got here so late in the day," added Aaron. "We got held up a bit crossing the Mississippi."

Craig looked concerned. The big river was just fifty miles west of him. "Trouble?" he asked.

Aaron shook his head. "No. There's a big trading post there now. We stopped to get an idea of what was going on." He cocked his head toward the scouts and Le Chenes troops around them, smiling. "Plus, the guys wanted to look at the girls."

Craig looked at him with interest. "A trading post, huh? What kind of stuff do they have there?"

Aaron shrugged. "Pretty much anything you can imagine. People have all sorts of things they either have extra of, have made, or have grown, and scavengers have brought in pretty much anything else you can imagine."

Augustus nodded. "You can trade for food, clothing, handmade soap, a cow or a haircut, and there's even a doctor and a dentist. Plus, boats have been coming in from both up and down river with trade goods."

"That reminds me," said Aaron, standing up. "I'll be right back."

Craig nodded to him, then looked at Augustus. "Where is it?"

"Up on 155 on the Missouri side," answered Augustus. "They have it set up pretty well. They even have security to take care of any trouble that might arise."

Craig nodded. "I've heard of a similar place up toward Kentucky, close to where a friend of mine lives. I've been wanting to go up there to see it, and him, but haven't been able to figure out how to do it."

"Why not?"

Craig looked toward the north as if envisioning the trip. "Well, it's over two hundred miles from here, on the other side of Nashville, and the most direct route would be straight between Nashville and Fort Campbell. I've heard that Nashville is a black hole that no one wants to go near and the area around Fort Campbell has become some kind of military state." He looked toward the house where his wife was probably reading a bedtime story to their son. "I just can't take the chance."

Augustus nodded. "I can understand that."

He thought for a moment. "Is this a good friend of yours?"

Craig nodded, remembering Zombie. "Yeah. We both had YouTube channels and kind of came together that way. We got to doing live streams together and became good friends." He looked at Augustus. "We even went up to Virginia's Lobby Day together. He became like a brother to me."

Augustus nodded thoughtfully. "And you say he's somewhere up around Kentucky?"

Craig nodded. "Up by the Kentucky line."

"Do you think he's made it through the mess?"

Craig smiled. "Oh, yeah. He had a nice farm and was even more prepped up than I was. Plus, he had just finished the police academy and had gone on his county's sheriff's department before the collapse."

Augustus looked at Craig with increased interest. "Sheriff's department, huh?"

"Yep. He quit being a truck driver so he could go into law enforcement. He said he wanted to make a difference with what was going on in the country."

Augustus nodded. "Sounds like a good man."

"Here you go!" said Aaron, emerging from the darkness back into the firefight and handing a brown bag to Craig.

Craig looked at the bag, then up at Aaron, then back at the bag. He reached out hesitantly. "What is it?"

Aaron smiled. "Sugar."

Craig's eyes widened. "Sugar?"

Aaron nodded. "Yep. Real honest to goodness sugar."

Craig took the bag into his hand, looking at it and feeling it's weight. "We haven't had sugar for almost a year." He looked back up at Aaron. "Where did you get it?"

"The trading post," said Aaron, sitting back down. "It came all the way up from New Orleans."

"New Orleans?"

"Apparently, sugar cane cultivation and refining has returned to Louisiana," answered Augustus. "They're starting to produce fairly substantial amounts and are delivering to trading posts along the Mississippi."

Craig looked even more surprised. "You mean there's river traffic and more trading posts on the Mississippi?"

Augustus nodded. "There seems to be quite a network working its way upriver from the Gulf. Kind of like what we read about in our history books." He shrugged. "I guess we should have figured this would happen. Communities have historically started on rivers and shorelines because of the availability of water and the easy transit of goods the waterways provide. I'd imagine it's happening pretty much all over the country."

Craig nodded. "I bet you're right. I never even considered that."

He looked at Aaron. "Any chance I could trade you for a little more sugar? I know Mrs. Peterson would like to be able to make some sweets."

Aaron smiled. "I already set a ten-pound bag on your doorstep."

Augustus tuned out, only hearing the other two men continue to talk in background fuzz as he looked around. The idea of making a trip from South Carolina to Kansas and back again would not even have occurred to him a year ago, but the resilience of the human spirit was an amazing thing and the number of functioning communities they had encountered was truly astounding. The cities were hell holes, as would be expected, and he was surprised to hear what Craig had said about Fort Campbell, but the growth of communities across the country gave him hope that a new start might be able to be made in the building of something that might resemble a new country. Le Chenes showed that. Stonemont and Jamestown showed that. The communities they had passed through on their trip had shown that, and the growing river trade and trading posts had shown that.

The key to creating a country out of communities was communication and commerce, and bringing more communities into contact with each other, just as Stonemont was doing in Kansas and Missouri, was important. And he realized that if it was being done elsewhere, it could and should be done in the South.

He looked back at the other men and waited for a pause in their conversation. "Craig, if it were possible, you'd like to go see your friend Zombie, wouldn't you?"

Craig nodded. "Oh yeah, but I can't leave my family here without me and I wouldn't want to take a chance on taking them on a trip like that."

Augustus nodded. "I agree."

He looked around at the men making their final preparations to bed down, then looked back at Craig. "There are a lot of communities growing across the country and it's important that we make contact and establish relationships with as many of the good ones as we can. It will give us greater communal strength and improve our lives through trade and social interaction."

Craig nodded. "I agree."

"I think it could be important to make contact with your friend. If he's what you say he is, I wouldn't be surprised if he has a strong community up there, and establishing contact with him could help us all."

He took a sip of his coffee before continuing. "I have a lot of men with me. How about I leave some here to guard your family while you're gone and have a couple of squads take you to your friend? When you're done up there, they can escort you back home, then all my men can make their way back to Le Chenes. If it works out, you've made contact with your friend and we've all made new friends."

Craig stared at Augustus, trying to process the proposal that had come so quickly. What Augustus said made sense, but the thought of leaving his family brought a sudden wave of trepidation. He felt his hand gripping his coffee cup tightly and looked down to see the liquid rippling from the tension.

The lesson immediately leaped to his mind that holding something tighter did not necessarily make it safer, but could simply cause internal disturbance. He consciously relaxed his grip and watched the liquid return to stillness.

He nodded to himself, then looked back up at Augustus. "Sounds good."

20

Christian gave two sharp raps on the door jamb before entering the den to see Jim and Mike looking down at a large map laid out on the center table.

"We were just getting ready to head into town," he said, "but Aedan said you wanted to see me?"

Jim looked up at him and nodded. "The scouts have found the ANK."

Christian's face grew dark. "Where?"

Jim motioned him over and put his fingertip on a spot on the map about midway between Topeka and Fort Riley. "Alma."

Christian looked down at the map, then up at Mike. "I didn't know the scouts were out that far."

Mike shook his head. "They're not supposed to be. A squad took a wrong turn on a sweep and ended up separated from their group. By the time they realized their mistake they were miles off course. Instead of retracing their route to their starting point, they took another wrong turn in an attempt to get to where they thought the group would be, but realized they were farther off course. They stopped and sent two scouts up a ridge to try to get reoriented. When they got to the top, the ANK was camped in a clearing below them"

"You mean they found them by mistake?"

Mike nodded. "Yep. A lost squad found them by mistake, somehow found their group again and they all high-tailed it back here." He shrugged. "Fortunes of war."

"And our guys weren't seen?"

Jim straightened up. "They were seen by one ANK sentry who they killed and took out of the area so he wouldn't be found. They say they can get back to the location and I've just told Mike to send five teams back there to keep an eye on them until we can get the rest on the way."

"The first five will be able to leave in a couple of hours," said Mike. "Twenty more teams will be able to leave tomorrow. Then we can see what we want to do."

Christian straightened back up. "We can't fight the whole ANK with three hundred scouts."

Mike shook his head. "No, we can't fight them straight up, but maybe there's a better way. We have to get eyes on target first. Then we'll see what we can do."

Jim walked over to the windows looking out onto the commons. "We're not into the real cold weather yet, but it's definitely cooling off. That always makes things a bit more difficult, especially for large groups without built-in support systems, and Tom thinks the ANK has been supporting itself mainly with raids since the new state doesn't have enough resources to keep it supplied."

"That means they're going to have to start increasing their raids in order to survive the winter," said Christian, "either going after larger targets or more small ones."

Jim nodded. "That's right."

"Which means the threat is increasing with the cold instead of decreasing."

Jim nodded again. "That's what I figure."

He looked at Mike. "George up in Wyandotte County says they picked up some ANK deserters coming east out of Topeka. Apparently, there's a new guy heading it up - some psycho that killed one of his own commanders as an obedience lesson to the others."

"Sounds like a real leader," observed Mike, derisively. "No wonder there are deserters."

Jim turned away from the windows. "Leadership through fear results in high desertion rates among the higher quality people and a retention of lower quality ones."

"And those with lower intelligence and psychiatric problems," added Mike.

Jim nodded. "Yep."

"That sounds like something we can use," said Christian.

Jim walked to the center couch and sat down, motioning the other two men to sit as well. "I think we can assume that the ANK does not have sufficient stores to support itself without constant raiding. The nature of their raids indicate that, and the information George got out of the deserters supports it."

He crossed his right boot over his left knee. "That means that, while their need to raid may increase, so too will the leader's hold on his troops weaken if their raids aren't sufficient to supply their needs."

"That's true," said Mike. "These guys aren't the men at Valley Forge. They're not fighting for something they believe in, and that makes their cohesion weak."

Jim nodded. "Groups like this coalesce around a strong leader who they believe in because they fear him and because he provides for their needs. When he stops being able to provide for their needs, their idolatry of him begins to wane and they begin to lose their fear of him. Then, the group fragments and crumbles."

"So, we just wait for that to happen?" asked Christian.

Jim shook his head. "We make it happen. Or at least help it to happen."

Christian looked at his uncle for a moment. "And how do we do that?"

Jim looked at Mike. "As soon as your first teams get up there, I want them to keep eyes on the main ANK encampment and shadow any ANK patrols or raiding parties. If possible, I want those patrols or parties wiped out once they're beyond the point of a quick response from their man body."

Mike nodded. "You don't want them to take any prisoners for questioning?"

Jim shook his head again. "Not yet. I want them wiped out. Take all their weapons and useable equipment, strip them of their uniforms and burn the uniforms in a fire large enough for the smoke to be seen from their main encampment. Then wait for a patrol to come investigate."

"And what do we do with them?"

"What's the area like?" asked Jim.

"The scouts said it's hilly with a mixture of woods and open spaces."

Jim nodded. "Good. If the group they send is small enough, same thing as the first. If the group is too large to take out easily, I want our people to stay in the trees and watch, but don't make contact. Keep taking out small groups until they send a large group. Then, we'll make a decision about the next step."

Mike smiled. "I like that."

Christian nodded. "So do I. It will put some fear in them. Plus, it might slow down their raids if they're worried about being attacked themselves."

"Hopefully," said Jim.

He looked back at Mike. "When the main body of scouts gets to the area, position them on the opposite side of the main body of the ANK, out of sight but within striking distance, and have them hold back until we take out the ANK patrols. ANK will be concentrating in the direction of our initial ambushes, and we'll look for an opportunity to attack their camp with our main body. We may not be able to take them all out, but we ought to be able to do quite a bit of damage before we have to disengage. Then, we'll see where we should go from there."

Mike nodded. "I like that even better."

"You really think our scouts can go up against the ANK?" asked Christian.

Jim shook his head. "Not straight up, but if we can take out some of their patrols it will create fear and uncertainty in the main body. Sufficient damage to the main body will increase that fear and uncertainty. They won't think they're the big dog on the block any more like their leader has made them think they are. That will start to shake their faith in him and start some fragmentation. Then, they have an enemy growing within their own ranks."

He rose from the couch. "For now, let's head to town to mix, mingle and make the big announcement."

"This should be interesting," said Christian as he got to his feet. "How do you think they'll react?"

Jim looked at him and shrugged. "I don't know, but I know it's going to be the next major step in our world.

21

Jim walked up the steps of the town hall and turned around to face the crowd gathered in the square. It was the largest crowd he had seen since the founding of Jamestown, as all those who lived within the Stonemont Autonomous Area had been invited to the outdoor Thanksgiving feast.

He had planned the announcement for this time, as the celebration would serve to remind everyone in attendance of the blessings they had enjoyed as a part of the larger Stonemont community, and, hopefully, engender in each of them a feeling of unity with and responsibility to the community that had made those blessings possible.

He glanced at Bill and Cassius Street who were standing to one side of him, then to Kelly and Christian who had followed him up the steps and were now standing on his other side. Looking back out over the crowd, he saw people migrating in from the side streets to fill in the space in front of the hall and could smell the last vestiges of the roasting steer that had fed the crowd throughout the day.

Children ran through the crowd, squealing as they played their chasing games that seemed to constantly change at the whims of the participants, and he could see some of the women setting up desserts on tables across the street for the crowd to enjoy after the announcement. He hoped that the fruit and berry pies made from the harvest of the Stonemont orchards would sweeten the taste of the news they were about to receive. In any case, he thought, it was going to be interesting.

He waited a few more minutes for the crowd to quiet, then raised his hands as if in welcome. "Happy Thanksgiving to you all! Did you get enough to eat?"

Applause erupted from the crowd, peppered by hoots, hollers and whistles.

Jim smiled. "Good! And by the looks of those ladies at the tables across the street there's more coming!"

Again, applause broke out, with several voices heard asking what was for dessert.

Jim laughed. "Well, I doubt that I'll remember everything, but I know there's pumpkin pie, apple pie, cherry pie, peach pie, gooseberry pie and chocolate cake."

"I'll have one of each!" called a voice from the back.

Jim nodded, chuckling. "I think I might, too."

He waited for a moment as the crowd settled down, then began to speak.

"We all have a lot to be thankful for, and we know that. Not long ago, the whole world fell apart and most didn't survive. We, however, did."

Murmers of agreement rippled through the crowd.

"We survived because we worked together, every person doing their part," he continued. "As a result, our communities are prosperous and safe and provide opportunities for everyone to live the lives that their abilities, interests, hard work and determination allow them to."

He paused for a moment, allowing that to set in their minds before continuing.

"God has blessed our work and we've been able to rebuild our lives in relative peace. Our home guard has kept us safe as they patrolled our border and our scouts have gone out repeatedly into the unknown world around us in order to make contact with other groups and try to secure larger areas that will maintain that safety.

"In most instances they have found other groups working together just as we are, but they have also discovered groups that pose dangers to us."

He looked around the crowd, seeing that everyone was now paying attention.

"Most of you are aware of an attempt by pre-collapse politicians and their hangers-on to establish a new state that they call New Kansas. They have organized an army they call The Army of New Kansas, made up of criminals and other misfits. They have raided towns to the west and south of Topeka, slaughtering the men and taking many of the women. Their raids are getting closer to us, and we believe we may soon have to defend ourselves against them."

A murmut rippled through the crowd and he waited for it to run its course and subside.

"Because of this new threat, and the possibility of similar threats in the future, we have decided to implement what we feel to be necessary measures to protect ourselves against them."

He looked at Kelly, then back at the crowd. "My wife has always had a knack for saying things directly. She brought this idea to me, and I've asked her to put it to you just as she put it to me."

Stepping away from the center of the steps, he extended his hand to invite Kelly to take his place.

Kelly stepped forward and looked out at the crowd. It was true that she had a way of speaking directly about things, and she wasn't shy about sharing her thoughts and opinions with those she came into contact with, but she had never been comfortable talking in front of groups - and this was a large one. Still, the words were what were important, and she couldn't let her own nervousness detract from the message.

"It's nice to see you all here," she started.

"We can't hear you!" yelled a man from the back of the crowd.

She quickly glanced over at Jim, who smiled and nodded, then looked back over the crowd, lifting her chin a bit in determination. "I'm sorry, I know I speak softly, but I'll try to talk louder!"

"That's better!" yelled the same voice, bringing laughter from some around him.

Kelly smiled. "Good, because what I have to say is very important."

She saw the hundreds of faces looking at her expectantly and for a moment wondered how she had gotten herself into this position, but continued.

"Like Jim said, we've been fortunate because everyone did their share. The safety that Stonemont provided allowed everyone to survive and prosper according to what they put into it and how hard they worked."

She took a deep breath, knowing the importance of what she was about to say.

"Now, it's time for every adult to step up and do their part to protect the communities they've helped build. The scouts and home guard have done an amazing job of protecting us up till now, but the fact that there are actual military forces possibly coming against us makes it necessary for everyone to be ready to stand up and be ready to defend their homes."

"What does that mean?" yelled a man in the middle of the crowd. "That we all have to join the scouts?"

Surprised at the challenging tone of the question, Kelly shook her head. "No, the scouts are a very special group. It takes a great deal of training and commitment to become a scout. What we need is for every adult to be a part of a home militia, ready to be called up when needed for community defense."

The crowd was mostly quiet, with a few mutterings floating through it.

153

"Does that mean women too?" asked a woman.

Kelly nodded. "Everyone except mothers of minor children."

The mutters increased and Kelly looked over at Jim again. He was not smiling this time and she turned back toward the crowd. "I'm sure that everyone understands the need and is happy to do their fair share to protect what they have."

"What *we* have?" shrilled a woman. "You mean what *you* have! You live in that big fancy house up on the hill! We live in houses made of mud!"

Kelly felt her face flush and a chill run through her body. She felt as if someone had punched her in the stomach and found it hard to take her next breath. Her mind seemed to freewheel in search of an answer to the woman's startling accusation.

Ever since first allowing people to join them at Stonemont, she and Jim had done their best to provide safety, security, and opportunity for those who came to them. Most had come from nothing, having been displaced from their previous homes and arriving with little more than the clothes on their backs. Many had children who would have faced starvation had it not been for the welcome and care they had received here. The idea that anyone would feel the kind of resentment expressed by the woman both confused and angered her.

She looked around the crowd trying to pick out individual faces, not sure who had yelled the accusation. "Who said that?" she asked, trying to keep her anger from making her raised voice shake.

The crowd remained quiet, most looking around at those surrounding them.

"I asked who said that?" she repeated, her voice louder with a hard edge to it. "*Somebody* said it! Raise your hand so we can all see who are!"

No one raised their hand and the crowd remained quiet.

She stood there, her confusion dissipating as her anger grew. "For any who feel that way, I have a question for you. Have you ever killed anybody to protect your family?"

The crowd remained silent and she shook her head in disgust. "No, you haven't, because you haven't had to," she continued, her voice getting louder. "The reason you haven't had to is because we provided safety and security for you. But I have!"

She looked over the crowd, her eyes blazing. "I shot a National Guard captain who thought he was going to take our food - the food you ate when you came to us. I shot him in the head at the dinner table on our veranda because he was pointing a gun at Jim. His blood and brains splattered the table. You can still see the stains on the stones where he dropped."

Muffled gasps peppered the crowd.

She paused for a moment, thinking of what else she could say that would impress upon the people the importance of standing up in defense of their community, then lowered her voice.

"We've all heard the saying that freedom isn't free, but it's easy to forget that when everything is good. Now, we all need to stand up and pull together to make sure we stay free."

She didn't know what else to say, then felt Jim's hand on her back. She looked up to see him smiling softly at her.

"Good job," he said quietly. "I'll take it from here."

She nodded, wanting to say more but relieved that she didn't have to, and stepped back to let him move to the center again.

He raised his hands. "My wife is exactly right, but I know that not everyone feels the same way. Tomorrow, we will be signing up anyone who wants to join the home guard at the town hall. We hope that many of you will. However, I don't believe in making people do anything they don't want to do. So, anyone who doesn't want to sign up certainly doesn't have to."

He looked over at Kelly, seeing a look of confusion on her face, winked at her, and turned back to the crowd.

"Right now, I bet all of the pie is sliced and ready for you to get your piece. So, Happy Thanksgiving to all of you, and may God continue to bless and protect us through the coming year!"

The crowd took a minute before it started moving toward the line of tables across the street and Jim watched it carefully. There was a decided hesitancy among many of the people, as if they weren't quite sure what to do, and the myriad of conversations combined to make an unintelligible hum.

He turned to Kelly. "You did a good job."

She didn't look at him, but continued looking at the retreating crowd, her face a mixture of anger and disappointment. "Did I? I don't feel like I did."

"You gave it to them straight. I couldn't have done any better."

She looked at him. "You would have made it sound better. You would have sold them on it. They would have been cheering when you were done."

He nodded. "That's why I wanted you to do it. I didn't want to sell them on it. This is too serious for that. I want each of them to make their decision on the straight information. That's what you gave them." He looked toward the crowd. "Now we'll see what they all do."

"What if a lot of them don't sign up?"

"Then we'll know."

"Know what?"

"Who we can't depend on. Who we can't trust."

156

She looked at him closely. "You expected this, didn't you? This is what you wanted to find out."

He nodded slowly. "I couldn't figure out how to do it. When you made your suggestion, I realized it was the perfect way."

She thought for a moment, then looked back at the crowd. "What if a lot of them don't sign up?"

He shrugged. "So be it."

"Not quite the response we were hoping for, was it?" observed Bill as he appeared at Jim's side.

Jim shook his head. "No, but pretty much what I expected."

Bill looked at him curiously. "Really? Why? I would have thought that most would feel a responsibility to help protect their own community."

Jim turned toward Bill. "Remember when I said that we wouldn't really know how people were until their lives were settled again?"

Bill nodded.

"Well, their lives have been settled for some time now. They aren't worried anymore about starving to death or being killed by raiders. Their lives are stable and safe because of what we have provided. Some probably understand that, but many probably don't."

He looked toward the crowd now lined up at the tables. "All of them will be enjoying pie provided by the Stonemont orchards. Tomorrow, we will find out who appreciates that and who doesn't."

"Separating the wheat from the chaff," said Cassius, who had also joined them. "An important step before making the bread."

Jim nodded. "Exactly."

"And what manner of bread are you preparing to bake?" asked Cassius.

Jim thought for a moment, then looked at Cassius. "A bread like was made in the old days. A strong, dense bread containing all of the life sustaining nutrients but without any of the modern additives meant to artificially preserve it."

Cassius smiled, understanding the message. "A good analogy. Wise intent, well spoken."

Jim held out his arm to Kelly. "Let's all go mingle and get a piece of pie."

They descended the steps and walked into the crowd, exchanging greetings with those they knew, nodding to those they didn't and occasionally stopping to talk for a minute with those who wanted to. By the time they reached the dessert tables, most of the people had been served and were either leaving or finishing up, chatting in small groups.

"Do you feel a slight chill in the air?" asked Bill, accepting a slice of pumpkin pie from one of the servers. "I mean, besides the one that usually attends late November?"

Jim nodded. "Sure seemed like it."

"Some people acted like they didn't want to talk to us," said Kelly.

Jim took a piece of Apple pie off a table, along with a fork, and looked around. "Well, if you want people to like you, give them things. If you want to see what they're really like, ask something from them."

Cassius nodded. "When Christ went away to pray on the night before his crucifixion, he returned to find the disciples sleeping. He had provided everything for them for three years, but in his hour of greatest need they couldn't even stay awake. Still, of the twelve, eleven found their strength and became powerful carriers of his message, even to the point of martyrdom."

"So, Jesus himself lost eight percent," said Bill, wryly. "How do you think we'll do?"

Jim looked at the quickly dissipating crowd. "I guess we'll find out tomorrow."

"Are you going to come down for the registration?" asked Kelly.

Jim thought for a moment, then shook his head. "No, I don't want anyone to feel pressured by me or any of the other leaders being here. I want an honest showing of where people stand."

He looked at Bill. "In fact, you might want to stay in your office and out of sight. The home guard officers can handle the registration."

Bill nodded. "You're probably right. How are you going to deal with those who don't register?"

Jim looked around at the quickly dwindling crowd. "I'll tell you day after tomorrow."

22

Jim looked over at Christian as he pulled onto South Street. "I forgot to tell you, a scout messenger came in late last night and said all of the teams are in place. Mike went back with him to direct things."

Christian nodded. "Good. Have they seen any ANK patrols come out from the main body?"

Jim shook his head. "Not yet."

"Maybe they're holed up for a while, hunkering down for the winter."

Jim shrugged. "Maybe, but our intelligence says they're thin on supplies. They're going to have to come out and raid if they're going to survive."

He pulled the Excursion over and parked in front of the town hall. "Have you seen the figures from yesterday yet?"

Christian shook his head. "Bill told us at dinner last night that it looked about even, but he didn't have a final count. How come you didn't hang around last night, anyway?"

Jim turned off the ignition and leaned back in the seat, watching several people walking into the hall. "I realized that it didn't matter. It's going to be what it's going to be. We're about to find out now, but things are about to change and what mattered to me last night was spending time with Kelly and the kids."

He looked back at his nephew. "You're going to find that out pretty soon. How's Naomi doing?"

Christian smiled. "She's doing great. We're both starting to get excited."

Jim nodded, looking out the window as if staring back in time. "I remember. We were excited even though we had no idea what to expect."

He looked back at Christian. "It's the greatest thing that will ever happen to you. It's the greatest responsibility you will ever have and it's the greatest joy you will ever have. You've got a lot to look forward to."

He turned to look out the window again. "You'll be confused, you'll be worried, and you'll even be scared. You'll know that you don't know what you're doing, but you'll do your best and your best will be good enough and it will get better. You'll make mistakes and beat yourself up over them later, wishing you could do things over again, but you can't, so just keep trying to be better every day."

Christian looked at his uncle. "Did you feel that way?"

Jim nodded. "I still do. I wish I could do everything again so I could do it better."

"You did a great job. You still are. Look at your kids. I hope mine turn out half as good."

Jim smiled. "Don't worry. With you and Naomi as their parents, they'll turn out great. You'll just always wish that you'd done a little better at some things. I guess that's just part of being a father."

He opened the door and started to step out, then stopped and looked back at Christian. "Your dad was a good man and a good father. You do it like he did it and your kids will be in good shape."

Christian started to say something but just nodded and got out of the truck.

Stepping onto the sidewalk, they nodded at several people they passed and turned up the approach walk to the town hall.

"They didn't seem too friendly," Christian observed.

Jim shrugged. "I guess we know what their decision was. They'll be less friendly when we tell them what the new deal is."

"So, you've decided?"

Jim nodded. "Yep."

"You want to tell me?"

"Let's get into Bill's office and I'll tell both of you."

They mounted the steps and entered the main doors to see Tracy coming out of the mail room.

"Hey, you two," she smiled. "You coming to see my dad?"

"If His Honor is free," smiled Jim.

She laughed. "He's busy drinking coffee and waiting for you. I'm getting the mail for him, so I'll go up with you."

Jim swept his hand in front of him, inviting her ahead of them. "Lead the way."

They took the stairs to the second floor and walked across an open area with large wooden beams supporting the high ceiling. Several doors were situated around the space, and they walked to one in the front corner that Tracy opened and breezed through.

"You've got callers, Mr. Mayor," she announced as she walked across the large office and dropped the handful of mail on the desk.

Bill turned around from where he had been standing looking out the window, his hands clasped behind his back.

Jim chuckled. "You look like Spencer Tracy."

Bill gave a small smile. "Which movie?"

Jim shrugged. "I don't know their names. One of them where he was worried about something."

Bill nodded. "That would be about right."

He walked to the desk and looked down at a yellow legal pad. "I've got the final numbers for you. Are you ready to hear them?"

Jim sat down in one of the two chairs facing Bill's desk and motioned Christian to take the other. "Yep."

Bill looked at him, then back down at the legal, saying nothing. Finally, he sat down and picked up the pad. He cleared his throat.

"We don't know exactly how many residents live in Jamestown, Church Crossing and School Center because we have never taken a formal census, nor do we document those who move in or leave. However, we estimate the total number to be around thirty-five hundred."

He cleared his throat again, still staring at the pad in his hands. "Of that number, we estimate that about half are children, bringing our registration pool down to about seventeen hundred, give or take."

He paused for a moment, then looked up at Jim. "Of that number, three hundred and thirty-eight have registered for the home guard."

Jim nodded. "Good."

Bill looked at him, confusion on his face. "Good? That's less than twenty percent. I expected it would be higher than that."

Jim shook his head. "We're seeing who's who and what's what."

He stretched his legs out in front of him, crossing his ankles and interlacing his fingers over his belt buckle. "Remember when we said that everyone was thankful for surviving the collapse, but the real test would be when things were good again? Well, things are good again and the test is here."

He nodded toward the window. "The fear of starvation and death is a distant memory for them now. They go to bed every night in a world made safe by those of us who have put ourselves on the line between them and a dangerous world they have forgotten exists, and they wake up to what they believe is the same safe world.

"They believe that what their daily lives have become is the new normal, and for them it is, but they have no idea what it's taken to provide that safety, what's out in the world beyond here or how quickly things can change. So, this is the true measure of the people. I'd say that if twenty percent of them are ready to stand up to defend their communities, that's pretty good. It's probably a lot higher than it would have been before the collapse."

Bill sat back in his chair. "But for only a fifth of the people to shoulder the responsibility of securing the safety of the rest is unfair if it's an entirely voluntary function."

Jim shrugged. "Do you remember our conversations about citizenship?"

Bill nodded. "You said you had decided against it."

"That's right. But there should be a difference in how those who are willing to stand up in the defense of the community and those who aren't are treated by that community."

He stood up and walked to the window, looking down on the street below. "Everyone has been given a choice. Nothing has been promised and nothing has been threatened, so each person's choice reflects what they have decided is right for them without any outside influence from us."

He turned back toward them. "Beginning on January first, those who live in our area will be separated into four groups - family, friends, guests and outsiders. Family are those who have been with us from near the beginning and have been an integral part of building our communities."

He reached into his jacket pocket and withdrew a folded piece of paper, handing it to Bill. "Here is a list of those considered family. You might have Tracy record them in the community record."

Bill accepted the folded paper, saying nothing but watching Jim.

"The second group are considered friends," Jim continued. "Friends are those who have actively contributed to the growth, safety and security of our communities, including all scouts, all home guard, those who have signed up for scouts or home guard and those who have established businesses or otherwise contributed their labor, knowledge or skills for the benefit of our communities."

"Who would that include?" Christian asked.

"Business owners and those who perform vital functions like the master gardeners, postal couriers and such. Kelly and Naomi are making up a list to give to Bill, which he and Tracy will review to make any additions they think are appropriate."

Bill nodded.

"That leaves the third group," said Jim, "the guests."

He turned back toward the window as if picturing those he was talking about.

"Guests are those who benefit from living in our communities but don't contribute beyond the work they do for the wages they receive, whether from Stonemont or any of the businesses. They have found a safe place to live but have given nothing, themselves, to help ensure that safety. They will now be required to contribute toward the security under which they are able to enjoy their lives in our communities."

"I thought you said you didn't believe in making people serve," said Christian.

Jim turned back to him. "I don't. Beginning on January first, there will be a twenty percent tax on all goods and services for those who are not family and friends."

Bill nodded, understanding. "That makes sense. Those who would not contribute of their own volition for the good of the community will now support those who do."

Jim nodded. "That's right. In the past, Stonemont has paid for all the wages, training, equipment and expenses of the scouts and home guard while the majority of the residents made no contribution beyond what they did for their own welfare. Now, everyone will participate in the process according to their own decision, with the taxes of those who work only for themselves paying for the protection and other benefits they get from the efforts of others."

Christian smiled. "I like that. I wonder if we'll get any pushback."

Jim turned and leaned against the deep windowsill, crossing his arms across his chest. "Oh, I expect we will. There's a certain class of people who think the rest of society should take care of them. We had them before the collapse and I'm sure we have them now."

He looked at Bill. "Wouldn't you say so?"

Bill nodded. "I wish we didn't, but I expect we do."

"So, what do we do with the complainers?" asked Christian.

Jim shrugged. "As long as they do their work, pay their taxes and don't cause any problems, I don't care. If they start making a fuss, they'll have to leave."

He tilted his head backward. "There's a whole wide world out there where they can make their own rules if they want to. If they want to live here, they have to go by our rules."

"And what if some want to join the home guard after they hear about the new tax?"

Jim shook his head. "That's just them trying to play the system. If they didn't want to do it for the right reason, I don't want them doing it for the wrong reason. We wouldn't be able to count on them."

"May I make a suggestion?" asked Bill.

Jim looked at him. "Of course."

Bill rose from his chair and walked to the window, again stuffing his hands in his pockets. "I wonder if there aren't a good number of people who would volunteer if they truly understood the necessity, but don't."

He turned his head to look at Jim. "The latter adult generations before the collapse were not raised to think very much about community service or obligation. Nor did most have any understanding of the real dangers of the world. They were raised to concentrate on their careers, ever-changing social issues and acceptance of everyone, regardless of how others differed from them in belief, values or world view."

"Diversity," said Christian, unmistakable contempt in his voice. "The vehicle by which the complainers gained control over the producers."

Bill looked at him and nodded. "Just so."

He looked back out the window. "We each construct our personal codes according to our own realities. Many of these people came from safe lives, through momentary terror, then to another safe life here, though a more difficult one than they had lived before. They have no real concept of the dangers surrounding them because they have been insulated from them by others."

He turned around to look at both Jim and Christian at the same time. "What if we could find a way to enable them to understand the necessity of service?"

Jim looked at him thoughtfully. "Like what?"

Bill gave a half shrug. "Well, I haven't thought this entirely through, and I could be wrong, but how about an emergency medical and services group to respond to things like the raids we've seen. Up until now, it's all been on the scouts. If there is going to be the kind of trouble we fear in the future, the scouts will need support units for dealing with casualties. It would be a way to introduce new realities to those who don't yet fully understand, and they would carry the stories back to their families and the community at large."

Jim and Christian looked at Bill, then at each other.

"I like that," said Jim.

Christian nodded. "Me too. It makes sense. Would we offer that as an acceptable alternative to the tax?"

"I would think so," said Bill. "And perhaps we could think of some other community needs that would be appropriate service as well."

Jim lowered his chin to his chest, thinking, then nodded slowly and looked back up. "Mr. Mayor, you've earned your pay today. Work with Christian to come up with any other community service you both agree to be appropriate. We'll announce them whenever you're ready between now and the first of the year and announce the tax at the same time."

He stood up from the windowsill and smiled. "I love it when I'm with people smarter than I am, but right now Christian and I have somewhere to go."

Christian stood up. "You didn't say anything about the fourth group, outsiders."

Jim shook his head. "Outsiders won't be allowed to live within our area. They can travel through, but they can't stay, and the tax applies to them since they will be enjoying the safety and benefits while they are here."

He started to walk toward the door them stopped, turning back to Bill. "We are a closed system. People can either become a part of us or they can leave. They can't stay within our borders unless they do it our way. Like I said, there is a whole world out there they can choose to live in if they don't like how we do things. If they want to be outsiders, they have to live outside of us."

They left the town hall and drove west from the square until they came to a road that looped to the south. The clear blue of the sky to the south and west was slowly giving way to the grey of clouds coming in from the northeast and they could feel the tinge of cooler air encroaching on the warmth of the sunlit valley.

"Do you come out here much?" Jim asked, looking over at his nephew.

Christian shook his head. "Not much. We came out a couple of times after we chose our homesite, but things have been a bit busy lately. You?"

Jim nodded. "I come out whenever I can." He smiled. "Now that you're doing more of the daily stuff, I have more time to sit around and think great thoughts."

Christian chuckled. "Is that what we're coming out here for, to think great thoughts?"

Jim smiled. "Well, we're coming out to talk. We'll see how great our thoughts turn out."

They drove across the valley, then entered the tree line on the eastern slope of the first hill. A few improvements had been made on the trail to the summit to allow for materials to be delivered for the new house, but they had to stay at a slow crawl for the Excursion's four-wheel drive to take the bites it needed to pull them up the hill.

After several minutes of negotiating the switchbacks, they exited the trees onto the open hilltop and stopped. The land swept away to the southwest until the horizon became a distant haze.

Christian whistled. "I'd forgotten what an amazing view this is."

Jim nodded toward a hill a mile to the west. "You're going to have a view just like it."

Christian looked at the distant hill. "It hardly seems real."

Jim opened his door and stepped out of the truck, grabbing a brown canvas pack from the back seat. "Let's go have a cup of coffee and talk about real."

They walked into the large open area toward a ring of stones bearing the soot of previous fires.

Christian nodded at the stones. "You *do* come up here a lot, don't you?"

Jim smiled. "Pull up a log and I'll get some coffee going."

Christian sat down on a log bench and watched as Jim got a fire going in the ring, poured water from a canteen into a coffee pot he had taken out of the pack and set it on a flat stone in the center of the ring next to the first crackling twigs. "I can see you do this often."

Jim nodded as he pulled two blue enamel cups and a small metal container out of the pack. "Yep, pretty much got it down."

He added more twigs, then larger sticks around the pot, took a burning twig and ignited spots around the encircling wood until the pot sat in the center of a ring of fire.

"I've never seen anybody do it that way before," observed Christian.

Jim straightened up, throwing the lighting twig into the fire. "That's 'cause I invented it."

Christian cocked his head and smirked. "You invented it?"

Jim chuckled. "Well, I never saw anybody do it before, so I must have. Of course, there might have been a bunch of other people invent it too, without me knowing about it."

Christian laughed as Jim sat down on a log bench across from him.

"Fifty years," said Jim.

"Fifty years?"

Jim nodded. "Yep. What do you figure you'll be doing in fifty years?"

Christian's eyebrows furrowed. "I hadn't really thought about it."

"Well, think about it. You'll be in your eighties. How many kids will you have? How many grandkids? What will they be doing?"

Christian shrugged. "I don't know. I guess we'll just have to wait and see."

Jim shook his head. "That's the way I did it for the first part of my life - until you came to live with me, as a matter of fact. It worked alright for a single guy in the *before* days, but it won't work in this new world for a guy starting a new family - not if he really wants to build something for his next generations. You have to think intentionally."

"Intentionally?"

Jim nodded. "We've been busy doing everything we can just to keep up, survive and establish some kind of workable society, and I think we've done a pretty good job."

Christian nodded. "I'd say so."

Jim looked out over the valley. "But that's not enough for the future. This is a time unlike any in our history. We are starting from almost physical scratch but with a wealth of knowledge in both history and technology. This is, perhaps, a once-in-history opportunity to decide exactly what we want the next world, our world anyway, to be. We must understand that, decide what we want to make of our world, and do everything we can to make it happen. Otherwise, the world will roll over us while we're just going along trying to live our lives."

"That reminds me of something you used to tell me when you started training me," said Christian.

Jim looked at him. "Yeah? What's that?"

"You told me that either I had to do life or life would do me."

Jim smiled. "Yep, that's about right."

"So, what you're saying is that we have to do the future, or it will do us."

Jim nodded. "You've got it."

Christian thought for a moment. "And how do we do that?"

Jim got up from the log and stepped over to the fire. "That's what I wanted to talk to you about."

He looked into the pot to see the water starting to bubble, took the lid off of the small metal container and shook some of the contents into the water. Re-capping the container, he put it back in the pack and sat back down on the log.

"Magic powder?" asked Christian, nodding toward the pot.

Jim chuckled. "Cowboy coffee."

"Cowboy coffee?"

"Yep. You toss grounds into simmering water, let it boil for a few minutes, take it off the fire and sprinkle some cold water in it to settle the grounds. Not fancy, but it's pretty good."

He pointed his finger to the horizon on his left and swept it around to the right. "We need to secure all of this for the future safety and security of our children and grandchildren - and their children and grandchildren."

Christian looked across the valley, letting his eyes scan from south to west. "Sounds like a day's work."

"And a half," nodded Jim. "It's not going to be easy. We have to change the way we do things - even the way we think about things."

Christian looked at him. "How so?"

"We've been playing mainly a defensive game, you might even say passive, only responding to things that we felt immediately threatened us. We were successful because we were against groups that were smaller than us. The new state and the ANK are different. They're larger than us and organized, at least to some extent."

"But they are definitely a threat to us."

"Yep, and it's up to us to deal with them."

Christian thought for a moment. "You don't think the other groups will help?"

Jim shrugged. "I'm sure they will to the extent they can. But that's the problem - to what extent can they?"

Christian nodded. "Yeah, not much."

"That's right. And we can't wait for them. We have to take care of it now."

Christian thought about that for a minute. "Wouldn't they be weaker if we waited until deep winter? After all, we figure they're already low on supplies."

Jim shook his head. "We can't take that chance. The longer we wait, the more raids they'll pull, and the more people will die. Also, if things get worse for them there will probably be defections, which would mean individuals or small groups of marauders that would be almost impossible to find. We'd just be going around cleaning up messes from now to forever."

"So, we take them all out at once?"

Jim nodded. "We try."

"And if we don't?"

Jim nodded toward the hill on which Christian was planning to build his house. "The future of your family, your kids and grandkids, depends on us doing it."

He got to his feet, stepped over to the fire and looked into the boiling pot. Taking a glove out of his back pocket, he lifted the pot out of the fire, placed it on the ground and took a second canteen out of the pack. "This is what does the trick," he said, sprinkling cold water from the canteen into the pot.

Waiting until he was satisfied the grounds had settled, he filled each cup with steaming coffee and handed one to Christian before sitting back down.

"Do you know what built America?" he asked.

Christian thought for a moment. "Courage, hard work, rugged individualism and faith in God."

Jim nodded. "And strong families."

He took a sip of coffee. "And what caused it's weakening and downfall? I mean, before the big *lights out*."

Christian thought back over his previous answer. "Well, I'd say fear, aversion to hard work, the development of a collectivist social attitude, a turning away from God and the weakening of families."

Jim nodded. "Bingo."

He took another sip. "The future will depend on whether we can re-establish the old ways."

He raised his cup toward Christian's hill. "You and Naomi have to raise a big, strong family. Mike and Tracy have to raise a big, strong family. Aedan, Brody and Morgan have to raise big, strong families. And they have to hold together because family is the foundation of everything else. That's where they will find their future security."

Christian looked at his uncle. "Arrows in the quiver, right?"

Jim smiled. "You remember."

Christian nodded. "Psalms 127. *As arrows are in the hand of a mighty man, so are children of the youth.*"

Jim nodded. "I missed my youth by a bit, but I did my share. The future is up to you all."

Christian looked at his uncle for another long moment, then lifted his cup in acknowledgement and nodded.

24

Malcolm Coates woke up to the sound of drizzle on the tent. It was getting colder every day, and the cold and wet matched his mood perfectly.

Food was getting low and the women who had been taken in the last raid probably wouldn't live out the week with the kind of treatment they were getting. When the food and the women were gone, he knew the men would be next to impossible to control. They had to run another raid.

He threw off the blanket and swung his legs over the side of the cot, a luxury he reserved to himself and his commanders, leaned forward for a minute to stretch his back, then pulled on his boots.

He sat there for a moment, listening to the drizzle and watching a drip in the opposite corner of the tent feed a rivulet that was fast approaching his cot. The temperature felt like it was in the mid-thirties, and that temperature combined with rain could be deadly. He had to get them out of tents and into permanent structures.

Standing up, he went to the door and unzipped it, then stepped out under the rain fly.

"Good morning, General," said a captain who had been standing close by under a tarp. "Did you sleep well?"

Coates looked at the captain. The man was a suck-up and about as worthless as the rest, but at least he did what he was told.

"Send a squad to recon that town down the road. Then tell the rest of the men we'll be moving there day after tomorrow."

The man nodded. "Yessir, General. Would you like some coffee? I just made some."

Coates turned toward a stand of trees he used as a latrine. "Just do what I told you to."

He heard the man say something he assumed to be "Yessir" and walked into a small stand of trees. This was his private space, a space everyone knew was off-limits to anyone but him, and he could almost forget that he was surrounded by an army of misfits while he was there.

The group had dwindled to somewhere around eight hundred over the past months, some having succumbed to illness, some on raids, some to violence within the ranks and some just disappearing into the night. The once formidable force, as least in numbers, had shrunk to a rabble of barely controllable losers and psychos who cared for nothing more than their next bite to eat or woman to torment. Thinking about them, he had half a mind to disappear himself and leave the worthless mob to its own collapse, but he didn't know where he'd go if he left. Maybe taking over the next town and getting into regular buildings would help to settle things.

Finishing his business, he walked out of the trees into the field dotted with hundreds of tents. Even fear of punishment hadn't been enough to get the idiots to pitch their tents in straight lines, and the myriad colors of the tents dotted the field in a hodge-podge with no discernible pattern. Smoke rose from many small fires, but he made his way toward the large fire in the middle, around which a number of men were gathered, a campaign tent pitched off to the side.

The men were dirty and unkempt, their once-matching uniforms now a collection of pieces picked up in raids either to replace damaged apparel or to satisfy some personal idea of victory over an essentially helpless foe. The toll of the last several months showed in their eyes, their mannerisms and the loose fit of their clothing that made them all look as if they were wearing the cast-offs of older brothers. The force he had once taken from the control of Briggs with a feeling of self-satisfied superiority now embarrassed him, as did the memory of his previous unshakable confidence.

"Mornin' General," said a man sitting on a backpack close to the fire. "Come to get yourself a little mornin' coochie?"

Coates looked at the man coldly, his anger rising at the man's question, tone of voice and smirk. Even a week ago, the man would never have dared to speak to him without rising to his feet, let alone implying that he had come to visit one of the women being kept in the large tent. "What's your name?"

The man's eyes narrowed but his smirk remained. "Chambers."

"Get more firewood."

The man looked at the fire, then at a large pile of wood next to it and back at Coates. "We've got plenty."

Coates opened his jacket, pulled his pistol from its holster, pointed it at the man's face and pulled the trigger.

The report of the pistol seemed dampened in the slow drizzle but was sharp enough to stop all conversation in the camp and draw attention to the circle around the large fire.

"Get to your feet!" Coates roared. "Every mother's son of you, get to your feet!"

Men throughout the camp slowly rose to their feet, those closer to the large fire more quickly than those farther away.

He looked around at the scraggly looking bunch. "We're moving out day after tomorrow to take the town down the road!" he yelled. "In two days, you'll be sleeping inside, have plenty to eat and have new women!"

A slow murmur drifted through the men, though without the energy he had hoped for.

"Those who do their jobs will be rewarded!" he continued. "Those who don't will be shot!"

A muffled female scream came from the tent.

Coates nodded toward the tent. "Take your last shots at 'em, then kill 'em. Captains to my tent in five minutes."

Merle Edwards stumbled over an unseen corn stalk , falling to his knees and catching himself with a hand that went wrist-deep in a puddle of freezing water. Regaining his feet, he snapped his hand to fling the water off and stuck it under his opposite arm to try to warm it.

"This sucks," he muttered. "Why the hell do we have to do this anyway?"

The man next to him shrugged. "Because the general told us to."

Edwards scoffed. "General? He ain't no general. He's just a psycho that shoots anybody who doesn't do what he says."

The other man nodded. "That's why we're doin' this."

Edwards walked a few more steps, studying the tree-covered hill in the distance. "What if we don't go back? What if we just keep on going? Plenty of others have done it."

The other man shook his head. "Where would we go? The general says we'll take the town and be sleeping indoors all winter. Food and women too."

"So he says," sneered Edwards, "but he's made promises before. Why don't we just go on to that town, take what we need and keep going until we find a place to hold up for a while? He'd never find us. He's never found any of the others."

The other man thought about that as he walked. "Maybe. You think the others would come with us?"

Edwards looked at the rest of the squad in front of them, making their way across the uneven corn-stubble field. "We'd have to kill Myers, but the rest would come, I think."

The other man nodded. "*You* gonna kill him?"

Edwards thought about that for a moment. He'd never liked the man Coates had given the squad leader position to. He was an arrogant little piss-ant who always got the favor of superiors because he snitched on others. The only reason he hadn't been fragged before was that nobody wanted to take the chance of being found out. The current situation took that fear away. He nodded. "Yeah, I'll kill him."

The other man walked in silence for a minute before looking at Edwards. "You have a plan?"

Edwards looked ahead at the hill they were slowly approaching. "It looks like we're going to be going over that hill. Once we get on the other side, they shouldn't be able to hear a shot from camp."

He took a few steps before looking at the other man. "Are you with me?"

The other man ran the scenario in his mind, weighing the options, then nodded. "I'm with you."

Edwards smiled. He'd been toying with this idea for a while and now the time and circumstance felt right. He looked up toward the hill again and quickened his pace.

24

The captain approached Coates' tent at a brisk walk, hurrying without trying to look like he was. He always liked to be the first to bring news to the general, unless, of course, it was bad news, in which case he made himself scarce.

"General!", he called, stopping just under the rain fly. "General, sir!"

It took a minute before Coates slipped open one of the flaps, revealing a woman lying on the floor of the tent behind him. "What is it?" he asked, bored irritation in his voice.

The captain risked a look at the woman, who was lying motionless. "I'm sorry to disturb you, general, but there's a report of smoke from the hill to our east."

Coates looked at the man. "Yeah? So what?"

The captain shifted nervously. "Well, as far as we know, there's nothing on that hill. Smoke probably means there's people there."

Coates gave a backward glance at the woman, then stepped out of the tent. "Did the squad check that hill?"

The captain shrugged. "I don't know. They're not back yet."

Coates looked at the captain sharply. "Not back yet? They should have been back hours ago."

The captain nodded nervously. "Yes, I was going to tell you, general, but...," he involuntarily glanced toward the tent, "well, you said you didn't want to be disturbed."

As irritated as he was, Coates couldn't argue with that. He had given instructions not the be disturbed. The woman was one he had reserved for himself and was still in fairly good shape. He had figured he could relax a bit before preparing for the move and had fallen asleep after his time with her.

The drizzle had stopped, but the grey clouds seemed to promise more and he judged it to be late afternoon. Whether the squad had gotten lost, met up with trouble or deserted was impossible to know, but he figured there was an equal chance of any of those.

He thought about the possibilities and considered his options. Sending another squad could simply repeat the unknown result of the first. Taking the entire body into an unscouted area could be dangerous and might leave them in an unsecured position. Neither option was ideal.

He looked around the camp, again disgusted at the sight. Trying to lead this rabble into any kind of operation was almost hopeless and the idea of simply walking away returned to him. He could take the woman, or not, and slip away at night without anyone knowing. By sunrise, he would be long gone, free again to plan a new start.

He looked at the captain. "Send three of the best squads to go find out. Have the men set up a heavy sentry line along the east side and tell them to pack up to move. Nobody sleeps tonight. Tell them we move out at dawn, and they'll be sleeping in warm beds tomorrow night."

The captain smiled and nodded. "Yes sir, general. Anything else?"

Coates looked out across the field and thought of his plan. He nodded. "I don't want to be disturbed till morning."

The captain looked at him oddly, but, thinking of the woman in the tent, felt he understood. "Yes sir. Have a good night general."

Coates watched the man walk away. Idiots could serve a purpose, and in this case, they would serve his.

Sending the best three squads after the first would get them away from camp. Setting a heavy sentry line on the east would leave the west side more open for him to leave through. And ordering no sleep for the troops would ensure them to be less effective than they already were in case he needed to deal with any of them.

He reviewed his plan in his mind to see if there was anything he had forgotten, then turned and went back into the tent.

Coates looked back at the body of the woman.

He had slept for several hours, then used the woman a final time. She had tried her best to please him, hoping to stay in his favor for the extra food and protection from the rest of the men, but her waning energy had left him dissatisfied and he decided she wasn't worth the trouble of taking her with him. There were other women out there.

Giving her a final whipping with his belt, both to satisfy himself and let anyone listening know there was activity going on in the tent that should not be disturbed, he slit her throat, cut an opening in the rear of the tent, and left.

25

Mike set the binoculars aside and picked up his rifle, bringing the scope to his eye to get a better look at the men coming across the field.

He had arrived the night before last and had immediately realigned the teams, placing the long-range shooters on the hill he was on and the strikers with the main body behind a hill on the other side of the main ANK encampment. Amazingly, they had found no outer ring sentries or roving patrols around the camp, indicating sloppiness, overconfidence, or both.

A waft of smoke from the smoldering uniforms behind him caught his attention as he focused on one of the men leading the group across the field.

The man was dressed shabbily, with a mismatching civilian coat and hat over BDUs he had probably been issued when joining the ANK. He wore fur-lined pac boots, apparently women's by the plaid pattern on the shafts, and had a single-sling sport pack slung over his right shoulder. The firearm he carried appeared to be an old pump-action shotgun.

That fit with the men they had killed. An unorganized and undisciplined group, the men had immediately fragmented when ambushed instead of forming any kind of concerted response. They had run, some trying to make it into the trees and some out into the field, but all with only one thought - trying to save themselves by running instead of fighting.

It had taken only a couple of minutes for the scouts to kill them all, then another half hour to strip them of equipment and uniforms and get the fire going. The weapons had been a hodge-podge of sub-par rifles and shotguns with only a couple of pistols among the bunch, and the uniforms looked as if they hadn't been washed since they were new. When one of the scouts asked him what they should do with the bodies, he thought about what the ANK had done to their victims and told the scout to let them rot where they fell.

It had taken longer than he had anticipated for an ANK group to respond to the fire, and it was neither another squad nor a group in force. Instead, it looked to be about thirty men moving across the field in only minimal order, some walking in clumps, some walking alone and some straggling behind.

Elevating his scope, he focused on the ANK main camp about a quarter of a mile beyond. Not a difficult shot for the long-range shooters with him.

He turned to the scout beside him. "Let the others know we'll start in a couple of minutes. Wait for my first shot, then take them all out. When they're all down, start putting fire into the camp."

The scout nodded and took off, staying low behind the ridge line.

Mike watched the men walking across the field, waiting until they were approximately three hundred yards from the hill. At that distance, the men wouldn't be able to make it across the open field to the tree cover or out of range before the scouts would be able to take them all.

He brought his rifle up.

His first shot took one of the lead men in the upper chest, causing him to stumble, then collapse after a stutter-step backward. The body twitched for a moment before remaining still and Mike swept his scope to another target as he heard rifle fire from the other scouts begin.

His second shot took a man in the top of the head as the man ducked to run, dropping him as if he'd been hit with a hammer.

Sweeping the field for a third shot, he acquired a man who seemed to have stumbled, then watched the man's head explode from the shot of another sniper.

Setting his rifle aside, he picked up the binoculars again to get a wider view of the field.

A number of men were down, lying motionless, while several were writhing on the ground. Rifle fire from the other scouts continued rhythmically and he watched men in field continue to drop.

Seeing a man toward the far side of the field turn and begin running back toward camp, Mike set the binoculars aside again, and again brought his rifle to his shoulder. Acquiring the running man in his scope, he tracked the man for several seconds, placing his finger on the trigger. Putting the first pound of pressure on the trigger, he waited for the moment to take a shot when a flash crossed his scope coming out from the camp.

Sweeping the scope to try to reacquire the flash, he saw more men coming out from the camp, some running and others seemingly backing into the field while firing their rifles in the direction of the camp itself.

Switching back to the binoculars again, he focused them on the ANK camp and saw more men running out of it into the field. Lifting his field of view to the hill on the other side of the camp, he saw the flashes of hundreds of rifles firing into the camp.

The slaughter had begun.

26

Sheriff Mark Freelove gave a wave to the guards at the contact gate and slalomed his pickup through the concrete bollards that had been installed to replace the original steel drums on the entry road. He was almost an hour late due to the latest raid against a family farmstead south of Carbondale, and the sickening feeling in his stomach was fresh enough to negate any of the positive feeling he usually had when coming to Stonemont.

Passing out of the bollards, he continued up the road and approached the entry gate where a group of men were working with two tractors.

One of the men stepped onto to road and held up his hand.

Freelove stopped, rolled down his window and nodded. "You guys look like you're working hard."

The man looked into the truck and nodded back. "Hey, sheriff. Yeah, Jim's having us take out the gate. He says it doesn't make sense anymore and people keep scraping their bumpers on it."

Freelove smiled, in spite of his bad mood, remembering a couple of times he had left some chrome on the concrete walls himself. "I understand. Can I get through? I was supposed to be here an hour ago."

The man nodded, waved at a man running one of the tractors, then turned back to Freelove. "You bet. He'll get out of your way. How are things out west?"

Freelove shook his head. "They've been better. How about here?"

The man shrugged. "Things are good. A lot of changes comin', from what I hear, but everything's good."

Freelove looked at the man with interest. "Yeah? What kind of changes?"

The man shrugged again. "Good changes for those who pull their weight. Not so good for others."

He stepped back. "Okay, you're clear. Have a good one."

Freelove nodded. "You too."

He entered the gate complex and slowly made his way through the switchbacks, determined not to leave any more chrome on concrete that would soon be gone.

Exiting the gate, he drove up the drive into the commons of the compound, parked next to the main hall and entered the building.

The hall was warm compared to outside and he walked through the entryway into the hall itself to see the others already seated at a long table drinking coffee. Roaring fires at each end of the hall explained the warmth and he unzipped his coat as he walked toward the table. "Sorry I'm late."

Jim rose from the table and walked to a side table on which a large coffee pot sat. "No problem, Mark. We're just getting started. Ken told us you've had a morning."

Freelove shouldered off his coat and hung it on the back of an empty chair. He nodded as he sat down. "I've had that."

Jim filled a mug from the pot and carried it to the table, setting it down in front of Freelove. "Well, I guess that's what we're going to talk about, mostly."

He returned to his chair at the head of the table and sat down. "Ken filled us in a bit about what he knew before he left you. Why don't you bring us up to speed."

Freelove took a sip of his coffee and looked around the table. Besides Jim, Christian, Mike, Bill, Tom, Kelly, Naomi and Cassius Street were there from Stonemont. Ken Dehmer, as head of the Kansas Rangers, was there with one of his men, and Sheriffs Rod McGregor and

Eldon White filled out the group. He took another sip, nodded and set his mug down.

"We had another farmstead hit last night. A family of three; husband, wife and daughter. Husband was killed, wife almost, and the daughter, well, she'll live."

He looked at his mug, took another sip while remembering the scene, then set it back down.

"The daughter tells us that three men broke in when the family was asleep. The father woke up and tried to put up a fight but was killed. The mother fought but was beaten and repeatedly raped until she was unconscious. The daughter was being raped when the mother came to and set fire to the house. That's what caught the attention of the deputy on watch who rousted some others to respond to the scene. When they arrived on the scene, the house was fully engulfed, and both of the women were lying on the ground outside unconscious."

"What about the men?" asked Jim.

"Found them after sun-up in a barn about a mile away. Killed them."

Jim nodded, looking around the table for reactions. All seemed to approve. "Good."

"It's the second attack this week," said Freelove. "Three last week, and we've had similar reports from other counties."

Jim looked down at his coffee cup. "It looks like we threw an M-80 into an ant hill."

Freelove shrugged. "There was no way to know that. If the ANK had stayed and fought, your scouts would have probably taken care of the problem once and for all. The fact that they broke and ran dispersed them in all directions, destroying any central control there may have been. It's caused a lot of smaller problems, but it stopped the bigger threat against towns by a large, unified group."

"That's right," interjected McGregor. "The smaller towns are now places of greater safety again because these smaller groups don't have the numbers to attack them. But people living out on farms and ranches need to remember that it's their responsibility to protect themselves."

"I agree," said Dehmer. "The Stonemont raid on the ANK changed the dynamics of the threat completely. It's gone from a military situation to a law enforcement situation - one we're becoming better able to address as we add more Rangers."

He looked at Jim. "Do we have any idea how many of them got away?"

Jim looked at Tom. "What have you been able to determine?"

Tom leaned forward. "After the action was over, the scouts did a fairly intense intel sweep of the area and the ANK camp. Kills were one hundred and eighty-seven. The number of tents and their contents suggests a total force of between eight and nine hundred."

"That's quite a bit less than what we figured they had," observed Freelove.

Tom nodded. "Our intelligence has shown an increasing desertion rate over the past few months."

"That coincides with the increase in crimes we've been seeing," said Ken.

Tom nodded. "That would make sense. As deserters left, they would need to find resources. The difference now is that while desertion over previous months was spread out over that amount of time and the areas they passed through, this has caused hundreds to explode into the surrounding area all at once. I'm actually surprised that we haven't seen more raids in the two weeks since the battle."

"There's been a marked increase in thefts and robberies since then," said Ken. "I'd guess they are responsible for most of it."

Freelove nodded. "Rod and I have said the same thing."

"How many Rangers do you have now, Ken?" asked Jim.

Ken looked at the other Ranger seated next to him.

"We currently have eighty-four Rangers on active duty with another couple of dozen going through the process," said the other Ranger. "It's enough to run patrols and handle investigations in areas without their own law enforcement capabilities, but not enough to be an effective unified force against a much larger threat."

Jim shook his head. "The Rangers shouldn't be expected to provide military service. Their role is law enforcement in the Republic of Kansas. If we feel we need a military element we need to address that separately."

Freelove nodded. "I agree. Which brings us to the subject of the Republic, or am I jumping the gun?"

Jim shrugged. "I'd say it all runs together." He looked around the table. "Does anyone want to stay on this topic, or are we ready to talk about the Republic?"

When no one else spoke up, Bill cleared his throat and leaned forward. "I agree that they run together, though I believe that we should return to this after discussing the larger issues."

Jim nodded. "Would you like to lay out the framework for everyone so we're all on the same page."

"Certainly," said Bill, looking around the table.

"As I believe everyone understands, a republic is a political entity in which the supreme authority is held by the people and their elected representatives. Many pre-collapse countries were republic's, including the United States."

McGregor scoffed. "If the people were the authority in the United States, I'm a rainbow armadillo."

Several heads nodded and Bill nodded. "Yes, I understand."

He looked at Jim, then back at those around the table. "What we are proposing is essentially a two-tiered government; a republic whose representative body is made up not of individual representatives elected democratically by other individuals, but by the separate elements of the confederation, each of whom conducts their political affairs according to their own chosen political system."

"Could you simplify that for those of us who like to use smaller words and shorter sentences?" asked McGregor.

Bill smiled, accepting the friendly chiding. "It's kind of like how The United States of America was supposed to be, or The Confederate States of America was, for that matter. Each state was designed to be sovereign in its own right, beholden to no outside authority for its internal affairs. Each could determine its own form of government according to what each felt was in its best interest. Each agreed to cooperate with the others in certain areas of mutual interest while retaining their right to separate from the confederation at any time and for any reason."

McGregor nodded. "So, each of our counties would be an equal part of the republic and we could run our counties however we wanted to?"

Bill nodded. "That's right."

"So, the Republic of Kansas would essentially be the confederation itself?" asked Freelove.

Bill nodded again. "Think of the confederation as being the group itself and the Republic as being the corporate entity through which the federation as a whole interacts with outside groups."

"What if a county wants to leave the confederation?" asked McGregor.

"Then they leave," replied Bill. "There can be no compulsion to stay, otherwise the entity would not be sovereign. However, leaving the confederation would mean that the group would be dealing with other groups, including the confederation itself, as an individual entity without the support or backing of the federation."

"What if an entity that seceded wanted to rejoin the confederation?" asked Kelly.

Bill looked at Jim. "That's not a situation we've discussed, but I would think it might be the same as allowing a new group into the confederation - unanimous consent by the member entities?"

Jim looked at him and leaned back in his chair. "That's an interesting question." He looked at Kelly and smiled. "Leave it to you to think of it."

He kept looking at her. "What do you think?"

"I think it depends on why they left," Kelly answered. "If it was to get out of a responsibility they had to the group, I don't think they should be let back in. If it was a difference of opinion over some policy or position, which they later reconsidered, maybe they should be let back in."

The group was silent for a moment, each looking at the others and waiting for someone else to speak. Finally, Bill spoke.

"I think this shows we have some things to discuss and decide," he said.

Jim nodded. "I agree. The order of business today is to decide whether we, as a group, a confederation, are ready and willing to establish the Republic of Kansas as a sovereign state."

He looked around the table. "I've stated my position before, but I'll state it again to give everyone a chance to express their opinion, for or against."

He took a sip of his coffee and continued. "I said long ago that Stonemont would remain sovereign and autonomous. I still hold to that position. Membership in the confederation, and thereby a political element of the Republic of Kansas does not preclude that. As with other constituents, Stonemont will remain responsible for all its internal affairs but will participate in the common defense of the Republic to the extent our resources allow. Also, we will contribute an equal share to the Republic for necessary internal operations such as the Rangers and basic government as is needed for the proper function of the Republic."

He looked around the table. "There will undoubtedly be a number of issues that will need to be discussed, but I believe that is the necessary basic agreement. The government of New Kansas is currently non-functional, the Army of New Kansas is nonexistent, and the capital is essentially void of any government. If we are to establish the Republic of Kansas and establish its capital at the State House in Topeka, now is the time. There may not be another."

The men and women at the table looked around at each other, then Freelove raised his hand. "I vote to do it."

McGregor raised his hand next. "I vote to do it too."

"I'm for it," said White. "And Ron Grey down in Bourbon County told me to tell you he was in too."

Jim nodded. "George up in Wyandotte county says they're with us, so I guess I will declare that the Republic of Kansas is now established, with the State House in Topeka as it's Capitol."

He looked around the table again. "Does everyone agree?"

Unanimous nods told him everyone did.

He turned to Bill with a smile. "Would you take care of constructing the necessary fancy sounding document for this?"

Bill nodded. "Of course."

He looked over at Street. "I wonder if Cassius would offer a prayer on this occasion?"

Street nodded and bowed his head, followed by the others.

27

Brandon heard the sound of a vehicle coming into camp and came out of his tent to see Samuel and Joseph getting out of Joseph's white pickup.

Jeremiah had led them south from Big Cedar into Arkansas, where they had stayed two nights in Harrison for Jeremiah to do some business, then headed east until one of the trucks had broken down just west of Pyatt. They had towed the vehicle into the small township and, with Jeremiah's intercession, had been allowed to set up camp in a small field behind the Dollar General.

That had been over a week ago and, while the locals had been watchful of them for the first few days, Samuel had arrived shortly thereafter, taking Jeremiah's place as their caretaker, and things with the locals had begun to smooth out. Two days ago, Samuel had brought Joseph with him to announce that they thought they had located an engine in Mountain Home they might be able to switch out in the truck that had broken down.

Brandon raised a hand to the two men as they walked into camp. "Samuel. Joseph. How are you all this morning?"

"Good," answered Samuel in his usual good-natured way while Joseph just smiled and nodded.

Brandon walked to meet them at the campfire, where a large coffee pot rested in the coals. "I was just about have a cup. Will you sit and join me?"

"Sounds good," said Joseph, walking over to sit in one of the canvas chairs arranged around the fire circle.

"Thanks," smiled Samuel, taking a seat across the circle from Joseph.

Brandon had seen the two do this the day before and had thought it strange until he realized they were watching each other's backs. These are careful men, he thought.

He put a glove on his right hand, took two metal cups off a row of hooks next to the fire and picked up the coffee pot. Filling each cup, he replaced the pot on the coals, handed a cup to each of the men, then got his own cup and sat down, looking at the other two.

Samuel was thick in the chest and shoulders. He always seemed to be at peace with himself, was slow to talk, almost appearing shy, but had a constant hint of a smile that implied he knew some secret that kept him in that quiet place.

Joseph was different. A bit shorter than Samuel, he had a walk and a stance that made him appear immovable, and an energy that seemed to be barely controlled lying just beneath the surface. His hands showed the strength of years of hard work and his eyes could go from jolly to deadly in an instant. Both men wore heavy boots and trousers, canvas jackets over hooded sweatshirts and stocking caps.

Brandon lifted his cup to them. "We'll be putting breakfast together pretty soon if you'd like to join us."

Joseph shook his head. "Thanks, but we already had ours." He took a sip of the coffee, the steam momentarily fogging his face, then rested the cup on his left thigh.

He looked at Brandon. "The guy in Mountain Home says he has an engine that will fit in your truck, but he says we'll need to tow it up there. Is that okay with you?"

Brandon thought about it. "Did he say what he'd want in exchange?"

Joseph shook his head. "It's taken care of. If you want us to, we'll tow your truck up to him and he'll switch out the engine for you."

Brandon looked at Joseph, confused. "You mean you'll tow our truck to Mountain Home, he'll replace our engine, and it won't cost us anything?"

Joseph took another sip of his coffee and nodded. "That's right."

Brandon continued to look at Joseph, trying to decipher what he didn't understand. "I don't want to sound rude, but why would you all do that?"

Joseph looked at him squarely in the eyes. "Are you familiar with the Golden Rule and the parable of the Good Samaritan?"

Brandon nodded, surprised. "Yes. It's one of the rules at Stonemont. The Golden Rule, I mean."

Joseph nodded again. "That's why."

Brandon tried to maintain his composure, working to manage the swift change from doubt to gratitude he was experiencing. He looked down at his coffee cup, then back up at Joseph. "All I can say is thank you, Joseph."

Joseph smiled and looked at Brandon closely. "You're welcome. Bye the way, I'm Joe Fox. I hear you've been looking for me."

Brandon tried not to show his surprise as he lifted his cup to take a sip. Although the revelation was sudden, it made sense. Samuel had taken over from Jeremiah, who had hopefully been leading them to meet Fox. After Jeremiah left, Samuel had spent a lot of time with them, getting to know them and becoming their interface with the local community. When Samuel brought Joseph into the mix, it had ostensibly been to try to get their truck fixed, and Joseph, in his quiet, friendly way, had gotten to know them well in a very short time. The soft interview that was invisible at the time was now obvious in hindsight. He smiled and nodded. "Nice to meet you, mister Fox."

Fox smiled. "Nice to meet you too, and you can just call me Joe. Joseph isn't even my real name."

He nodded toward Samuel. "And you can call him Sam. I just thought we'd use the Old Testament sound to do a bit of misdirection."

Brandon nodded. "Yeah, with your beards and your names I thought you were Mennonites or something."

Sam chuckled. "We're something, but we're not Mennonites."

Brandon looked at each of the men. "Well, Joe, Sam. Thank you again for all your help."

Fox nodded back. "Our pleasure. So, what did you want to see me about?"

Brandon started to answer but stopped as a Viking approached Fox and spoke quietly in his ear.

Fox listened for a moment, then turned back to Brandon.

"I have to go take care of something. We'll be back later and bring dinner. Then, we can talk."

Fox waved off the scout making his way around the circle with the coffee pot. "Thanks, but we have to be leaving in a minute."

Dinner had been good, consisting of a goat stew with vegetables and fresh bread the Vikings had brought back, and now they were relaxing around the fire.

He looked over at Brandon, thinking about the question the younger man had just asked. "We don't discuss specifics like numbers, locations, methods or operational considerations, but if your boss is just wanting to make contact with like-minded people, I think we can talk."

Brandon looked around the fire-lit circle at the mixture of scouts and Vikings. Unknown to him or the other scouts, they had been under surveillance by a crew of Vikings since Jeremiah had brought them into Pyatt, a revelation that had brought him a combined sense of both safety and unease. The thought of the term *crew* reminded him of a question that had been playing around the edges of his mind and he looked at Fox. "I was wondering why you call yourself Vikings. We have a motorcycle club up our way who call themselves Vikings, but that's not what you all look like."

Fox smiled. "No, we're not." He took a sip of his coffee. "I was in the Army and did most of my time in Special Forces. A lot of the other teams had cool sounding names and I thought we should have one too, so we decided to call our team Vikings." He took another sip. "I just kind of kept rolling with it, and when I started a YouTube channel I needed a name, so I called it Viking Preparedness. It caught on, and when I started a Patreon channel I called the subscribers Vikings."

Brandon looked at him. "Are all of your people from your YouTube and Patreon channels?"

Fox shook his head. "A lot of them are, but a lot of them came from the Viking network we developed before the change."

Brandon had heard some of this but wanted to hear it from Fox himself. "How did you go about building a network?"

Fox looked off into the darkness, remembering. "I always figured something like this was going to happen. I tried to get people to understand the importance of preparing and I used my channels to try to teach them what I thought they needed to know. The channels grew quite a bit and I soon had viewers from all over the country - all over the world, actually."

He looked back at Brandon. "I knew that when everything fell apart it would be important to have as large a support group and communication system as possible, and I thought that with Vikings all over the country we might be able to help people form groups that would provide that support for them, so I started what we called Viking meet-ups where people could get together, meet others, form relationships and hopefully build their own groups to give themselves that support."

He took another sip before continuing. "We ended up having quite a few groups form around the country and a lot of them have been able to stay in touch since the collapse. It's been good for the groups themselves and for others they've been able to help."

"Like us," observed Brandon.

Fox smiled and nodded. "Like you."

Brandon looked around the circle again. Firelight illuminated the faces of the scouts and Vikings who had co-mingled during dinner and were now involved in their own conversations. They would leave soon to relieve their counterparts manning the security ring and he observed that it would be difficult to tell the difference between the groups if he didn't know his own men. He turned back to Fox.

"They're trying to re-structure some kind of government up our way. Are they trying anything like that around here?"

Fox shrugged. "I've heard some talk. Does your boss support that?"

Brandon shook his head. "Jim says that Stonemont won't be under any outside government again."

Fox nodded, understanding. "Have you ever heard of *The Fate of Empires*?"

Brandon nodded. "I heard Mike talk about it. He said he'd heard Jim talk about it."

"Are those your bosses?"

Brandon nodded again. "Mike is head of scouts. Jim is the big boss."

Fox chuckled. "That was the name of a Bruce Lee movie, *The Big Boss*."

He took a sip. "*The Fate of Empires* was written by a British Army officer named John Glubb. Glubb explained that empires go through a cycle of about two hundred and fifty years from beginning to end. The United States was in collapse when this happened, right on schedule. It's too early to know what will replace it, but something will."

Brandon looked at him. "You think so?"

Fox nodded. "As much as we might not like to think it, government of some kind is necessary. It's the nature of man. Unfortunately, it's also the nature of man to screw things up. It's just the way it is. Man has a sinful nature."

Brandon thought about that for a moment. "What do you think the next kind of government will be?"

Fox shrugged. "Who knows? It's going to be a mess. Everyone will have different ideas and too many will want to be in charge. Power will eventually begin to centralize in different places, then someone will want to expand their control over others and the trouble will start over again."

He stood up. "We'd better get headed back. We'll come by in the morning to tow your truck to Mountain Home. It'll take them a couple of days to switch it out, so we'll have time to talk some more."

He drained his cup and handed it to Brandon, who had also gotten to his feet. "Things are secure here, so you can rest easy. Thanks again for the coffee. We'll see you in the morning."

28

Brian Crockett removed the saddle from the paint and set it on a saddle stand outside the stall. The filly was coming along nicely and with a little more work would be ready for the kids to ride. That would mean six horses that could be ridden by anyone - a goal he had been working on since before everything had crashed.

He gave the filly a quick once-over to check for any new scrapes or cuts, something he always did after riding in the woods, then led her to the rear door of the barn, removed the bridle and set her loose into the pasture.

He watched for a minute as the filly trotted toward her mother and siblings halfway across the field, then swung the door shut and turned back into the barn.

Snow had started to fall shortly after daybreak, and his fields and the woods beyond were starting to hold the cover. It was a sight he loved, and he stood there for a moment thinking about the years he had lived here - the years that generations of his people had lived here. There had been good times, but there had been tough times too. It had taken a lot to weather the bad times, but his family was still here, and he intended to keep it that way.

Life since the collapse had actually been easier for him than life before. Though most of the conveniences of the modern world had disappeared, their disappearance had taken things back to the old ways, ways of hard work, personal responsibility, integrity, and self-reliance. He had been raised that way, and so had many of his family and friends. They had done alright. Others hadn't been raised that way and most of them were gone. It had made life simpler.

The sound of an approaching engine drew his attention to the road and he saw Chase Williams' black pickup slowing down and stopping at his gate, giving a couple of courtesy taps on the horn to let the house know that company was here.

Brian hung the bridle outside the filly's stall, exited the barn and started walking toward the house as he watched Chase get out of his truck, open the gate, drive through, shut the gate behind him and drive up to the house.

Smoke rose from the chimney, and he saw the back door open and close quickly as his wife threw something to the dogs.

Williams parked the truck next to the house and got out, seeing Brian walking toward him. "I s'pose you thought you were going to get the day off!"

Brian waited until he got within conversation distance. "What's up?"

"There's a big bunch of hard looking men at the church who say they want to see you."

Brian squinted at him. "Me? What for?"

Williams shrugged. "They just said. *if you know Brian Crockett, you get him down here, and you get him down here right now.*"

Brian looked at Williams closely, sensing there was something Williams wasn't telling him. "Who are they?"

Williams started to smile. "Well, there's some boys from South Carolina flyin' the battle flag and some other boys from Kansas flyin' the Pine Tree flag." His smile got bigger. "And there's some guy with them who says he knows you, name of Craig Peterson."

Brian's squint quickly turned into a half-smile at the mention of his friend's name. "Yeah? What's he look like?"

"Kind of a serious, intense looking guy with glasses and a beard and wearing a stocking cap. He told me to mention the Virginia rally to you, and to tell you he was stayin' the course, keepin' the faith and that this was the flip side."

Brian's half-smile grew larger as he heard the take on his old sign-off and he nodded. "That sounds like Craig. Give me a minute and I'll follow you back."

It took him just a couple of minutes to grab his rifle and tell his wife where he was going, then ten more to drive to the church.

Rounding the bend, he saw the small field next to the church filled with neatly parked vehicles. A number of Southern Cross and Bonnie Blue flags waved from antennas and flagstaffs, with a few Pine Tree flags flying from several vehicles on the end. Slowing down, he followed Williams as they turned off the road and into the church's parking lot.

Pulling up next to the church and putting the truck into park, he turned off the engine and stepped out.

Several groups of men milled around the lot and he scanned the groups. Then, seeing a small group of men walking toward him, he recognized his old friend in the lead and started walking to meet them.

As they approached each other, their smiles grew in recognition and greeting.

Coming together, they embraced each other. After a moment, they separated and held each other at arm's length.

"Good to see you, man," said Brian, his voice tight with emotion. "How did you get up here?"

Craig looked around at the Le Chenes and Stonemont people around him, then back at Brian, his eyes moist. "Well, it's quite a story. Got a minute?"

"There were surprises," said Brian, shaking his head, "a lot of surprises."

He laid his fork aside and looked across the table at Craig. "A lot of people I thought would stick just curled up and died or blew away." He shrugged. "Some others that I thought would never make it found something deep inside themselves and stood up when it counted."

He took a long drink from his water glass. "Funny world."

News of the arrival of outsiders had spread quickly and people from the community had swarmed the church once the nature of the visitors had become known.

The women of the community had soon organized a potluck dinner that rivaled some of the largest pre-collapse church events and the men had gathered to meet and share information with the group, eager for news from beyond the area.

With more people than the church would hold, a bonfire was built outside for those who wanted fresh air, and soon the locals and the visitors were mingling like old friends.

As the man the visitors had come to see, Brian had taken a large round table in the corner of the fellowship hall where he now sat with Craig and the Carpenters and the Stonemont team leaders.

Although he and Craig had tried to catch up with each other, the activity of the afternoon had left little opportunity for more than superficial exchanges. Now, things had settled down a bit and they were serving themselves from platters and bowls of fried chicken, cornbread, mashed potatoes with gravy and fried okra. He looked at Craig. "How are things out your way?"

Craig shrugged. "It's a mixed bag. We're okay where we are. We have some neighbors who work together pretty well, and a small community several miles away, but you don't want to go anywhere near Memphis or anywhere west of us, really. I'd say we're on the rim of where it starts to get a bit iffy."

Brian nodded. "Same around here. You don't want to go anywhere close to Nashville, or Fort Campbell, for that matter. As a matter of fact, I'm surprised you got up here the way you did without running into trouble."

"We kind of threaded the needle," said Augustus. "We took back roads to split the distance between Nashville and Fort Campbell. We heard about both."

Brian nodded again. "You heard right and you got lucky. Campbell has spread a pretty wide web since this all happened and has kept a tight clamp on everything in their area. We've even had refugees show up here from over there."

"Refugees?" asked Craig. "You mean from around Campbell?"

"Yep. They refer to themselves as escapees."

"Why?" asked Aaron.

Brian took a thick piece of cornbread off a platter and began to butter it. "Martial law. They say they liked the security the Army provided at first, but the rules got more and more restrictive with work requirements, curfews, and such. They said it became almost like a prison."

He took a bite of the cornbread. "The first few families left with no problem but then they put in travel restrictions and started stopping people from leaving. After that, it changed from leaving to escaping."

Craig looked at him incredulously. "The U.S. Army holding people against their will?"

Brian swallowed the bite of cornbread and shrugged. "It's not the U.S Army anymore. Even if it was, they've done it before around here. Remember the Civil War?"

He shook his head. "No, it's just a fort run by authoritarians trying to control whoever they can."

"Like the FEMA camps we used to talk about," observed Craig.

"Yep," Brian answered, accepting a platter of fried chicken from Augustus on his right, taking two pieces and passing it to Craig on his left. "A lot of the things we used to talk about have come true, haven't they?"

Craig took two pieces from the platter and passed it on. "Are you worried about them trying to expand closer to you?"

Brian took a bite of chicken and chewed it thoughtfully before answering. "Yes and no. The *no* because they've apparently been losing people. We've heard from some people in Kentucky that some of the soldiers have deserted, though we don't know how many. The fact that you all got through might mean that they've pulled their outer patrols in a bit, which could mean they're getting shorter on people."

He paused to take a drink of water. "In the *yes* column, people who want to control other people often want to control more people, which means expanding. I guess we'll know in time."

He looked at Augustus. "How are things down around you all?"

Augustus thought for a moment. "We're secure in our area. Some of the bigger landowners have formed a confederation of sorts covering a large part of the western Carolinas, northeastern Georgia and part of Virginia. There's even been talk of re-forming the Confederacy."

Brian looked at Augustus closely. "Really?"

Augustus nodded. "That's the discussion."

Brian looked at Craig. "That would be something, wouldn't it?"

Craig smiled. "Yes, it would."

Brian looked back at Augustus. "Are they talking about including whole states, or parts of states, or what?"

Augustus shrugged. "There's talk both ways. Some would like to keep the original states intact for ease of identification and administration. Others have suggested that new boundaries might make sense in order to form smaller states to bring government closer to the people.

208

One thing that is being discussed is keeping the cities out of it."

"Out of it?" asked Brian. "What do you mean?"

Augustus nodded at Craig. "Like you and Mr. Peterson were saying, the cities are a mess. Nobody wants them in the new Confederacy. They suck all of the good out of the country and all they give back is trouble."

"And what are they going to do with the cities?" Brian asked.

Augustus shrugged. "I don't know. Let 'em rot, I guess."

A young girl came over to the table and put her hand on Brian's shoulder, smiling shyly at the other men.

"Daddy, mom said to tell you that Mr. Peterson's room is ready, and you can come home whenever you want."

Brian patted the girl's hand. "Thank you honey. Tell her we'll be home in a bit."

"Okay, daddy."

He watched his daughter walk off, love and pride plain in his eyes.

"Do you have more children, Mr. Crockett?" asked Augustus.

Brian nodded, still watching his daughter. "Yep, two more girls and a boy."

He looked back at the men around the table. "They're the reason we have to make sure we do things right, them and others like them. We can't let things go back to the way things were, and we can't let regional warlords rise up and threaten us."

Augustus nodded. "I couldn't agree more."

Brian looked at Craig. "Well, Miranda's excited to see you, and the kids are too, so let's get you over to the house as soon as we finish up here."

He looked around at the others around the table. "You all stay as long as you like, make yourselves at home and make sure you get seconds on pie. The ladies will be mighty upset if you don't."

29

Patrik could feel the reverberations of the heavy drums as he walked through the tunnel to the small inside arena of the auction barn. They had been fortunate to capture some of the slavers this time - fortuitous for him, but not for them, and it was what he had been waiting for.

He lowered his head a bit to make sure his antlers cleared the door header as he stepped into the arena. The antlers were a last-minute thought, and according to one of his men were more Celtic than Viking. That wouldn't matter tonight. Their purpose was to increase terror and he was sure they would do that.

He stepped into the arena and the drums stopped, leaving only the crackling of the pitch torches to accentuate the sudden silence. One of the hanging men let out a choked whimper.

Walking to the center of the arena, he surveyed the scene in front of him. Six men hung by their wrists from railings around the elevated viewing stands, leaving their bound feet hanging several feet above the loamy dirt and sawdust floor. Light from the torches reflected off their naked bodies and rivulets of stress-sweat ran from their necks to their toes. One had already urinated from fear.

Above them, his men filled the tiered rows of benches, watching the scene below.

Observing the men suspended before him, he looked inside himself for any feelings of human empathy but found none. Time after time they had arrived at the scene of a Muslim massacre, only to be able to bury the slaughtered, and each time the horrors had increased. The men hanging in front of him had participated in those slaughters and now the manner of their deaths would serve as a tool for the defeat of their brethren.

Spreading out his arms, a large knife in one hand and a sickle in the other, he lifted his face as if to the heavens and began singing an ancient Viking chant of victory and death.

He knew the picture he presented to the captives, the antlers adding two feet to his already immense frame and the woad on his face and body emphasizing his many intricate tattoos.

He continued chanting until he heard another whimper and stopped suddenly, focusing on the one who had made the noise. He had found the weakest one.

Dropping his arms, he walked slowly toward the man. He smiled. "You all have been killing Christians. You have tortured them, slaughtered them and enslaved their women."

He turned so that all could hear him and raised his voice. "You have committed these atrocities in the name of your religion, the one you claim to be a religion of peace, and you have been able to because of the passivity of the Christians you have met."

He spread his arms again turning slowly so that all could see his war paint. "But I am not a Christian."

He shook his head slowly. "No, I do not forgive. Rather, I bring justice. I bring death. I bring wrath upon those who attack the innocent."

Again, he lowered his arms, scanning the hanging men. "Two of you will live to tell the story of what you see tonight. Two, so that one will not lie, for you are a people of lies."

He observed the hope that arose in the eyes of the weak one, the hope that he would be one that lived.

Walking to the one he recognized as the strongest of the group, he looked up into the man's eyes. "Ready to meet your virgins, tough guy?"

The man started screaming something at him in Arabic.

With a flick of his wrist, Patrik dug the point of the scythe into the man's groin, twisted and pulled.

The man's screams became animalistic and momentarily distracted the others from seeing his severed genitals on the floor leaking blood into the sawdust.

Patrik watched with interest as the man bucked and thrashed in agony, his screams eventually subsiding as shock began to set in.

He nodded. "I bet that hurt, Abdul, or whatever your name is, but I'm sure you'll be interested to know that's not the worst thing I'm going to do to you tonight."

Patrik stepped around the pool of blood under the man's feet and walked to the next man, whose eyes were filled with terror. "I guess his virgins are going to be awfully disappointed, don't you think?"

He looked down the line of men. "Who here speaks English?"

"I do," answered the weakest one, his voice trembling.

Patrik shook his head in disgust. "Hell, you *all* do when you *want* to, don't you? Better speak up now. If you can't speak English, I don't need you alive."

"I do!" Exclaimed another one.

"Me too!" yelled a third.

Patrik nodded as the remaining two both acknowledged they could speak English. "Not in such a hurry to get to your virgins now, huh? Well, we'd better keep going."

He walked to the second man. "So, Abdul number two, did you enjoy torturing those men, burning them alive and raping the women?"

The man began to wail. "No, no, no! I do not do it! I do not do it!"

"Bullshit," said Patrick, plunging the sickle into the man's groin and severing his genitals.

The man screamed and thrashed as the first man had, his bound wrists and ankles restricting his movement as blood spurted from his groin onto the ground.

"We'd better step this up a bit if we're going to get everything done before you boys bleed to death."

He quickly castrated the third and fourth raiders, ignoring their screams as he stepped in front of the remaining two.

"You two pay close attention. I'm going to let you live and you're going to go back to your tribe and tell them exactly what you saw here."

He stepped back and raised his voice so that the others might be able to hear them through their shock and pain. "I hear you all don't like pigs. Well, you don't know what you're missing; bacon, sausage, pork chops ...," he shook his head. "Wow."

He walked back out into the center of the arena. "But you know what? After all those years of being eaten by us, I bet those pigs are *pissed*! I bet they'd like a chance to eat some of *us*! What do you think?"

He looked at the four castrated raiders who were crying, choking and wailing. "What do you think, guys?"

"Hey, Abdul!" he yelled at the first raider. "What do you think? You think pigs might like a chance to eat some of us for a change?"

He shrugged. "Well, let's find out."

He walked over to the side of the auction floor and opened a gate.

The snorts preceded the first pig that entered the floor, followed by nine others.

The pigs scrambled around the floor, excited by the smell of fresh blood and soon set upon the severed genitals lying in the sawdust.

A feeding frenzy erupted as the pigs fought for their shares and Patrik moved to the side of the floor, ascending a set of steps to the viewing level.

"Boy, those pigs are hungry, aren't they boys? Probably because they haven't eaten in a few days. Better give them some more."

With that, he leaned over the rail and plunged his knife into the first raider's abdomen, ripping it upward and then side-to-side.

The raider's intestines extruded through the cross-shaped wound, pushed out further by the man's thrashing until loop after loop began to fall out.

"Your guts are falling out onto the floor, Abdul. Better go try to put them back in."

With that, Patrik cut the rope binding the raider's wrists to the rail and the man fell onto the arena floor.

Further excited by the new meat, the pigs tore into the downed raider, tearing chunks out of the screaming man as blood sprayed over the frenzy.

Turning to the remaining raiders, Patrik repeated the process on the next three raiders then looked at the remaining two who were watching in horror.

He grabbed the weakest one by the hair and jerked his head up to look him in the eyes. "Remember. And tell your friends I'm coming for them."

30

Jim awakened to a feeling of emptiness. It was still dark, and something didn't feel right.

He rolled from his right to his left side and stretched out his hand, only to feel an empty space on Kelly's side.

He lay there for a moment, thinking about the day ahead. The decisions had been made and the preparations were in place. If all went well, the Republic of Kansas would take its place at the Capitol in Topeka before sundown. If things didn't go well, there was no telling what would happen.

He threw the covers off and let his mind run through the possible scenarios while he showered, shaved and got dressed, carrying his boots and gun belt down the stairs and into the kitchen where he found Kelly standing at the sink and looking out the window.

He stood there for a minute, watching her quietly until, sensing his presence, she turned around.

"You're up early," he said quietly.

She looked at him and nodded. "I couldn't sleep."

He walked toward her. "Something on your mind?"

She leaned into him as he put his arms around her. "You know what's on my mind."

He gave her a squeeze and kissed the top of her head. "Everything will be fine."

She stayed still for a moment, then straightened up, keeping her hands on his waist while looking up at him. "Then why can't I go with you?"

He smiled. "Because you have to stay here with the kids."

"And why can't the kids come, if everything is going to be fine?"

"Because they have school."

She swatted his arm as she stepped away. "You let them skip school for everything else."

He nodded, stepping toward her and putting his hands on her shoulders. "I know. It's just that we'll have a lot of things going on today and the fewer people who are there, the quicker we can get everything done."

He kissed her on the forehead. "We'll all take a trip up there in a couple of weeks when we can enjoy ourselves"

She looked up at him and started to say something but stopped herself and turned back to the counter. "Do you want some breakfast?"

He hung his gun belt on the back of a chair and sat down. "Sure. What do we have?"

"What do you want?"

"Chocolate cake."

She turned and looked wryly. "We're out of chocolate cake."

He feigned surprise. "We are? Who ate it all?"

She rolled her eyes."You did. About a month ago."

He shook his head. "Well, we obviously need more chocolate cake. Okay, I'll have bacon, eggs and hash browns."

"Pancakes too?"

He shook his head again, slapping his stomach with the palm of his hand. "Better not. Bikini season will be here soon."

She laughed. "Okay."

He sat down and pulled on his boots, then stood back up poured himself a cup of coffee from the pot on the stove.

"Bill still doesn't want to be president. He was still talking about it when the meeting broke up last night."

She shrugged. "I don't blame him. He'd have to be away from home and deal with all the political idiocy. Who would want that?"

He sat back down. "Yeah, but I explained to him that it should just be a part-time job, and it's important that we have someone dependable and impartial in the position, and someone who won't let the position go to their head."

"Then why don't you do it?"

"Because I'm not impartial." He took a sip of his coffee. "Besides, I don't want be away from home and deal with all of the political idiocy."

She smiled, putting a large cast iron skillet on the stove. "I guess he's as smart as you are."

He laughed. "It's just going to be a figurehead job, for the most part. He'll still be able to live here and just travel up there occasionally. Plus, everyone agreed he's the right one for the job."

She began laying thick slices of bacon in the skillet. "But won't he have to be up there to do all of his official work?"

He shook his head. "There shouldn't be all that much official work. That was the problem with the old world - too many government officials and bureaucrats making up a bunch of work which made a bunch of trouble for the people."

He listened to the bacon start to sizzle. "Which reminds me, how is the situation with the so-called citizens' council coming?"

She took a second skillet off a rack and placed it on the stove. "Well, *the contribute or pay taxes* plan has made their numbers explode. It seems like a lot of people don't like it."

He watched her put a dollop of lard in the second pan. "That's what I figured."

She spread the quickly melting lard around with a wooden spatula, then deposited several hands full of shredded potatoes into the pan. "It will be interesting."

He nodded. "Yes, it will."

He cocked his head at the stove. "Do you really think I can eat all of those hash browns?"

"Christian is coming to breakfast."

"Oh. Did he tell you that?"

She shook her head as she put a basket of eggs on the counter. "No. He's walking over here now."

He looked through the window at the darkness. "You've got good eyes."

She turned around and looked at him. "I do, and I can see right through you."

He mocked surprise. "You can?"

She nodded, her face growing serious. "Uh huh. You don't want us to go with you because you think there might be trouble."

He pursed his lips in thought, not wanting to brush off her concern but not wanting to elevate it either.

"I wouldn't say that I think there might be trouble as much as I'm just recognizing the possibility. Things could get a little hinky and I don't want you all around if it does."

He smiled. "I want you all to be able to come up to the new capital once everything has been settled and secured so that we can make a nice day of it."

She continued to look at him, trying to find a crack into which she could insert a convincing argument, but found none. She nodded and turned back to the stove. "Okay, but you'd better not get shot again."

He shook his head. "I won't."

"You won't what?"

Jim turned to see Christian coming in the kitchen door.

"Sneakin' around and eavesdropping again, huh?"

Christian smiled. "How else am I going to know what's going on around here?"

"He said he won't get shot again," said Kelly, turning the bacon. "And I don't like the fact that you're not going with him."

219

Christian walked over to the counter and took a cup off a rack. "Neither do I, but you know how reasonable your husband can be."

Jim chuckled. "Bill, Tom and Mike are going. In fact, Mike's already up there on the security ring. With me up there, that's a majority of the Stonemont core. You two have to stay here."

Christian filled his cup from the coffee pot and sat down across the table from Jim. "I get it. But getting it and liking it are two different things." He took a sip. "When are you taking off?"

"Whenever Bill gets here. I told him to come over about sun-up. A scout team is meeting us at the contact gate."

"And when are you coming back?"

Jim shrugged. "I'd like to come back tonight if everything goes well. If not, then tomorrow."

Christian looked toward the window looking out onto the commons. "I wonder how The President slept last night."

Jim laughed. "He was still grumbling about it when we said goodnight."

He looked closely at Christian. "I'd like to have Naomi up there with us, but I just don't want her around any possible trouble right now."

Christian nodded. "She understands, and I agree with you. I hear Aedan wanted to go."

Jim took a sip. "Yeah. I thought about it, but it's not time for him yet."

"How many eggs for you two?" asked Kelly.

"Three please," answered Christian.

"Three for me too, honey," said Jim. "Thanks."

Kelly forked the cooked bacon out of the pan and laid them on a drip rack. Pouring most of the grease into a jar, she cracked six eggs into the pan and turned the hash browns.

"You're not having any?" asked Jim.

Kelly shook her head. "I'll wait and eat with the kids."

She looked at Christian. "I want to spend the day in town with the kids. Would you and Naomi like to go with me?"

Christian shrugged. "Sure, I don't think we have anything special going on. Any particular reason?"

She glanced at the eggs, the looked back at Christian. "Have you seen the latest numbers for those who have signed up for service?"

Christian nodded. "About sixty percent."

Her eyes narrowed. "That means twenty percent aren't on board. That's a lot of people living among us who could start a lot of trouble. I want to get a feel of the people around town. I think we're going to have to deal with this pretty soon."

She turned back to flip the eggs. "Okay, top off your coffee and get your plates. This will be ready in about one minute."

31

"I still think the term *administrator* would be more appropriate," said Bill as they approached the contact gate.

Jim looked over at him. "What kind of Republic has a head of state called the *Administrator*? Does everyone remember Sam Houston as being the *Administrator* of the Republic of Texas?"

Bill shook his head. "No, but I'm no Sam Houston, and look how long that lasted. Maybe Texas would have remained its own Republic if he had been called the administrator."

Jim smiled as he slalomed the Excursion through the bollards and waved at the guards. "Yeah, right."

He nodded ahead. "There's our escort."

He pulled abreast of the lead scout vehicle and stopped. "You all ready to escort the President?" he called over to the team leader riding shotgun.

The scout smiled and nodded. "Yes, sir. If you'll fall in behind the second truck, we're ready to go."

Jim nodded, waited as the scout vehicles started up, then fell into the middle position with two trucks behind him.

He glanced over at Bill again. "You don't mind if I hum Hail to the Chief, do you?"

They took the route through Lyndon and Carbondale, the same route he and Christian had travelled when they had taken Ralph to Topeka to get Rebecca, Becky and Bobby on the day they had met Mark Freelove, and he reflected on the time that had passed since then.

He never would have dreamed what would become of his once peaceful home, or the many challenges and changes that had come along, and he realized that he would never have been able to plan it if he'd had to. It all just seemed to have happened, to have fallen together on its own as a natural evolution of situations.

There was no doubt in his mind that, although his basic preparedness had been the foundation, God had been the orchestrator of things, the director of all that had happened, and that his own part had simply been to do the basic and proper things as different needs presented themselves.

He looked over at Bill and thought about how instrumental the man and his family had been in the development of what Stonemont and its satellite communities had become. He thought about the hours they had spent talking over coffee, bourbon and dinners about law, justice, philosophy, society, and the nature of mankind, and how each had helped enlighten the other in areas of their own expertise. The relationship had expanded the knowledge and understanding of both.

"I want you to do for the Republic what you have done for Stonemont," he said.

Bill gave him a questioning look. "And what is that?"

"To guide the legalities according to morality."

Bill thought about that for a moment. "So easy to say and so difficult to do."

Jim nodded. "I know. But if the Republic has any hope of succeeding, it must have a moral foundation to support it. You're the man to do it."

Bill was silent for a moment. "And when the foundation has been laid, may I then go retire in my home on the mountain?"

Jim smiled and nodded. "Yes, you may then go retire on your mountain."

Bill envisioned the land hold he and Ann had selected and smiled. "Good."

32

Approaching Topeka, they exited the highway onto Topeka Boulevard.

The area appeared desolate, the industrial buildings sitting dark as if long forgotten and debris fluttered in the fences along the roadside.

"This might sound strange," said Bill, looking out his window, "but I just had a sudden thought of Ohio and wondered if it looks like this." A touch of sadness crept into his eyes and voice as he remembered his former home. "I imagine it does."

Jim looked over at him. "Probably. I occasionally try to imagine what cities like New York, Chicago and Philadelphia must look like now. When I start getting down to the details I have to stop."

Bill nodded slowly. "Yes. I think I'll stop too."

The convoy turned into the entrance of the airport and followed the escort who had been waiting for them around to the parking lot across from the Combat Air Museum where a number of scout vehicles were parked. Seeing Mike step out from a group of men and hold up his hand, they stopped.

"Got a surprise for you," Mike said as he walked up to Jim's window.

Jim looked at his head of scouts. "Yeah? Good or bad?"

Mike shrugged. "Weird. The city's a wreck, but we can't find hide nor hair of the ANK or anything else that looks like security."

Jim kept looking at Mike, thinking. "Are you sure?"

Mike nodded. "We've made multiple sweeps and some deeper probes into the outer areas, and they seem to be gone."

Jim thought for a moment. "What about the Capitol?"

Mike shrugged. "We haven't been inside the building, but there's no security around the outside that we could see. We have a security ring about six blocks out and roving patrols out farther."

He cocked his head at the far end of the parking lot. "Freelove, McGregor and White are over there waiting for you. Ken Dehmer's at the Capitol with some of his Rangers."

Jim looked over at Bill. "You ready?"

Bill shook his head slowly. "I have no idea. But the time is here, and we must each do what is ours to do."

Jim smiled. "Less than inspiring, but I guess it'll have to do."

He looked back at Mike. "Okay, let's go."

They met briefly with Freelove, McGregor and White, then formed up into a convoy with the rest to enter the city.

Like the outskirts, the city was deteriorating, with greenways and vacant lots overgrown with weeds and grass, debris littering both roadways and open areas, and vacant buildings collapsing in their dormancy from lack of attention. Abandoned cars sat dust-covered along the sides of the road and small packs of dogs could occasionally be glimpsed running between buildings.

Things became more congested as they made their way farther into the city. The industrial outskirts had changed to residential neighborhoods, and they saw an occasional person looking furtively out a window or watching from the corner of a house.

"It's worse than the last time we were here," observed Jim.

Bill watched the passing houses with disbelieving eyes. "I can't imagine what they've been through. How can people live like this?"

Jim looked out his side window and saw a thin young girl in an oversized coat, her arm around the shoulders of a younger boy, watching them from a front porch as they passed. "It's all they know."

Bill nodded sadly. "We must help them to know better."

They passed a scout checkpoint, Jim returning the half-salutes offered by the men, and continued toward the center of the city where they soon saw the towering dome of the Kansas State House.

Jim nodded toward the massive building. "Your new office, Mr. President."

Bill looked up at the looming building but said nothing.

Breaking out of the residential area, they entered the government sector and soon pulled up along the curb on the south side of the Capitol grounds.

Jim looked over at Bill. "Last chance to back out. The Commissioner for Pet Licensing job is still open."

Bill looked up at the Capitol building again and nodded. "I'll take it."

Jim chuckled as he opened the truck door and stepped out. "Sorry, you're over-qualified.

Bill stepped out of the truck and met Jim on the sidewalk where they were quickly surrounded by their security detail. Looking up, they saw the familiar figure of Ken Dehmer descending the steps from the Capitol's south doors and walking toward them. Looking around, they observed scout teams at each intersection around the Capitol grounds.

Dehmer walked up to them briskly, stopping several feet away. "I'll have to say, I think this is the strangest day of my life."

Jim nodded and looked at the new white Stetson on Dehmer's head. "Trade in your skimmer?"

Dehmer offered a small smile. "A Trooper's a Trooper. A Ranger's a Ranger. I thought we'd show a little solidarity with our friends down south."

He looked at Bill. "The Governor's in his office waiting for you."

Bill looked at Dehmer, confused. "For *me*?"

Dehmer nodded, then looked at Jim. "When we went up the steps to set security at the entrance a man who said he was the governor's assistant came out and said the governor was waiting for us. I went up and spoke with him for a few minutes. The building is secure and he's waiting for us in his office."

Jim looked at Bill, then back at Dehmer. "Okay, let's go."

They walked to the main sidewalk of the Capitol where they were joined by Freelove, McGregor and White, then mounted the massive steps to the south entrance.

Nodding at the sentry holding the door open, they entered the dim entry hall.

"His office is on the second floor," said Dehmer, nodding to one of two brass and marble staircases. "Follow me."

Their footsteps echoed off the stone walls as they ascended the stairs to enter an upper hallway where they saw other scouts posted. An inconspicuous doorway in the corner displayed the word GOVERNOR on the transom window above the door and Dehmer led them to it.

Following Dehmer through the door, they stepped into a richly appointed reception area to see a sad looking man standing behind a desk on the right side of the room.

They stopped and the man gave a slight nod.

"The governor is waiting for you in his office," he said quietly.

Looking at each other, Jim, Bill, Freelove, McGregor and White followed Dehmer into the back office to see a man seated behind a large desk.

The man looked frail, his eyes showing a weariness that only came with physical disease or prolonged mental stress. He rose from his chair, his suit hanging on his thin frame as if it belonged to a larger man. He nodded. "Gentlemen."

Jim, Bill and the sheriffs nodded back as Dehmer stepped aside.

"Your friend has advised me that you are the leadership of the new Republic of Kansas," said the man.

Jim nodded. "We are."

He nodded at Bill. "This is our president, William Garner."

The man nodded slowly. "President Garner. That has a nice sound to it."

He looked at Bill. "We tried to rebuild a state that would return a decent life to people." He looked out of the window as if remembering. "At least, I thought that's what we were doing."

Bill nodded. "I'm sure you did."

The man looked back at Bill. "Perhaps you will have better luck."

He looked at the other men, then back at Bill. "I wonder if I might have one more minute alone?"

Bill read the message in the man's eyes and wondered if he should try to dissuade him. Finally, he nodded, turned and left the office, followed by the others.

They waited in silence in the outer office, each understanding both the sadness and the enormity of the moment, until they heard the single gunshot.

33

"Do you think we can make the master bath look like that one on Pinterest?"

Jim smiled as he got up from his chair and walked to the campfire. "Which one?"

"The one with the huge wooden beam going across the shower."

"Oh, yeah. I remember."

He picked the coffee pot full of hot cocoa off the coals and carried it to her. "I guess we could, if we could remember what it looked like."

"We don't have to remember," she said, holding her cup up for him to fill. "I have a picture."

"You have a picture?" he asked, his smile growing larger as he filled her cup.

She nodded. "Uh huh. I printed it off before all this."

He filled his own cup and chuckled. "Always thinking ahead, aren't you?"

"I try."

She took a sip of her cocoa and pulled her collar up as she looked out across the dark valley. A full moon and a canopy of stars allowed her to see for miles.

"Do you think we'll sit here and watch the night sky when this is our front porch, or will we get too busy again?"

He sat down in the camp chair next to her. "I'm sure life will try to make us too busy, but we have to try not to let it." He took a sip of his cocoa. "That's why I've got all of these other people doing things."

He smiled at her. "Pretty sneaky of me, huh?"

She laughed and raised her cup toward a hill on the other side of the valley. "Is that where Christian and Naomi's place will be?"

Jim nodded. "Yep."

"It was nice having everyone close together in the compound, but it will be nice to have our space again, with just the kids."

He smiled at the thought. "Yes, it will."

She was quiet for a moment, thinking how to phrase something that had been in the back of her mind.

"Do you think things will settle down now that the Republic has been established?"

He shrugged. "Maybe, maybe not. Time will tell."

"I'm just hoping the kids will be able to grow up in peace."

He shook his head. "There will never be peace. It's just not in the nature of man. We have to always be ready to fight for the freedom we have now, because there will always be those who will want to take it from us."

She shook her head. "I just want for us to be able to enjoy the blessings God has given us."

He nodded, looking down at his cup. "Thomas Paine said that those who expect to reap the blessings of freedom must, like men, undergo the fatigues of supporting it." He took a sip. "Few generations have avoided undergoing some of those fatigues if they wanted to stay free."

He looked over at her and saw that she was staring up into the sky, deep in thought. "Do you want to head back after this cup?"

She continued looking up at the stars, watching their sparkle in the night sky, and shook her head. "No. Let's stay here a while longer and enjoy the peace. Who knows what tomorrow will bring?"

Made in United States
Troutdale, OR
06/08/2024